A Cat of
One's Own

A Cat of One's Own

An Alice Nestleton Mystery

Lydia Adamson

A DUTTON BOOK

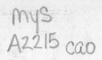

mys
A2215 cao

DUTTON
Published by the Penguin Group
Penguin Putnam Inc., 375 Hudson Street, New York, New York 10014, U.S.A.
Penguin Books Ltd, 27 Wrights Lane, London W8 5TZ, England
Penguin Books Australia Ltd, Ringwood, Victoria, Australia
Penguin Books Canada Ltd, 10 Alcorn Avenue,
Toronto, Ontario, Canada M4V 3B2
Penguin Books (N.Z.) Ltd, 182–190 Wairau Road, Auckland 10, New Zealand

Penguin Books Ltd, Registered Offices: Harmondsworth, Middlesex, England

First published by Dutton, an imprint of Dutton NAL,
a member of Penguin Putnam Inc.

First Printing, February, 1999
10 9 8 7 6 5 4 3 2 1

 REGISTERED TRADEMARK—MARCA REGISTRADA

Library of Congress Cataloging-in-Publication Data is available on request.

Printed in the United States of America
Set in Transitional 521
Designed by Eve L. Kirch

PUBLISHER'S NOTE

This book is printed on acid-free paper.

Chapter 1

It was the last day of November. Cold and sunny. A minute before the noon hour.

I was standing on Beekman Place—a very posh Manhattan neighborhood south of Sutton Place, north of the U.N., and fronting the East River.

I was staring at a lovely row house.

The question to be posed is not, What is Alice Nestleton doing here, but, What is Amanda Avery doing here?

I was on Beekman Place to see her. She had called me out of the blue. The last time I had seen or spoken to Amanda was almost five years ago, in Northampton, Massachusetts, where I was involved in an ugly little episode with a group of classical musicians known as the Riverside String Quartet.

Amanda had helped me out then. When I saw her that last time she had just been fired from Smith College, where she had been teaching drama and literature while living a life of genteel poverty.

She was still absorbed in her never-ending critical work on Virginia Woolf and still trying to interest me in her never-finished one-woman play based on Woolf's diaries.

Now, Beekman Place?

She had obviously moved far and fast.

I rang the bell. She answered the door very quickly, as if she had been waiting for me anxiously. We laughed and embraced.

"You look wonderful, Alice," she said.

So, in fact, did she. Amanda was a small, strong-featured woman with close-cropped gray hair. Her hair had turned irretrievably gray when she was in her early thirties, and that suited her just fine. I'd never known her to have a man, a pet, or a vice. She was dressed now as she always had dressed in the past—like a bohemian sculptor with a mile-long scarf and thick, vengeful sandals.

But the moment I entered that beautiful duplex apartment full of French country furniture, with windows on the river and on the street, I knew something had changed in Amanda's life.

Because I saw a dog.

It was an old Gordon setter bitch who didn't even get up—she just thumped her tail happily.

One rarely sees Gordon setters in the United States.

They are bigger than their English cousins and much harder to keep in the average city apartment.

"That's Good Girl," said Amanda.

"Since when did you become a dog lover?" I asked.

"She belongs, really, to Ivan."

"Ivan?"

We sat down. Amanda served coffee and blueberry muffins and cleared up the puzzle: she had married a wealthy shoe manufacturer from Massachusetts two years ago. His name was Ivan Tasso. He had died suddenly, six months ago, from a blood clot on the brain. This, I realized, was his apartment, or one of them, and Good Girl had been his dog.

"He was a rare man, Alice. Intelligent, passionate, funny. A kind of Don Quixote. But the only thing he could do right was produce shoes."

"Better that than windmills," I noted. I felt a bit awkward. It wasn't the kind of conversation I had had with her in the past. We had never been intimate friends. We had talked mostly about the theater.

"He did a lot for me, Alice," she said. "And now I want to do something for him."

I squirmed in my chair and sipped coffee from the oversized Provençal mug. What did she mean? The man was dead. And why was she telling me this?

I changed the subject. "Have you been living here long, Amanda?"

"Two years."

"You're joking! You mean you've been in Manhattan for two years and you never gave me a ring till now?"

"I meant to, Alice. Really, I did. It was just that—well, there were some bad times. Oh, don't get me wrong. I loved Ivan and the marriage was wonderful. When I say things were bad, I mean things were bad for me professionally. My project was going nowhere. I couldn't think anymore. I just . . . well, I began doing foolish things and—"

She stopped talking there, walked quickly over to me, and grasped my hands. "It is so good to see you again, dear." Amanda began pacing then, and talking very fast. "Ivan had a premonition that he was going to die, Alice. He asked me to do something for him after he was gone. He wanted me to get a friend for Good Girl. Because he knew she'd be lonely."

We both stared at the beautiful beast, who was still lying peacefully on the rug. Once again she thumped her tail. Good Girl kept her big soulful eyes trained on Amanda. The dog had that classic Gordon setter frame: rangy, gaunt, with large tattered ears; her coat was a soft black with creamy tan markings.

"When you say a 'friend,' Amanda, do you mean another setter?"

"No. A cat. Ivan made it clear I was to get a cat."

"But why?"

"Ivan's father was an onion farmer. He had a lot of house

4

pets. As a puppy Good Girl was raised with kittens. She loves them."

"Yes, that's quite common on farms," I said.

"Can you get one for me, Alice?"

"Oh, sure. I'll keep my ears open. I'll call you the minute I hear of a little one who needs a home."

"No!" she said vehemently.

It startled me. "What's the matter?"

"I want a cat now."

"Now?"

"Today. Immediately. I've procrastinated long enough— six months. I don't feel very comfortable with animals, Alice. I never have. But this is an obligation. This is something I *have* to do. Understand?"

"I suppose so, yes. Listen, Amanda. There's an animal shelter just ten blocks from here. It's called Abide. I could take you there and help you get a cat."

A little maliciously, I added, "After all, that's what cat-sitters are for."

"Would you, Alice?"

"Of course."

She was hovering over my chair. "Where is this place? Shall I call a taxi?"

"Can I finish my coffee first?" I chided her.

She laughed. "Sorry, dear. Take your time." But she was already clearing away the milk pitcher and brushing at the muffin crumbs.

*   *   *

I'd heard a lot about Abide. Many people I knew had adopted pets from that shelter.

But I had never been there and I wasn't prepared for the reality of it. It was a large, busy, and efficient place, dazzlingly clean, where the staff was fiercely protective of its waif boarders.

Amanda and I walked into the reception area and were greeted by a young woman in a red smock. Soon the rather severe-looking interviewer appeared. She led Amanda to a corner spot where she grilled her unsparingly about her motives for adopting an animal. Presumably the aim was to weed out those would-be adopters who were sadistic maniacs, or not able to provide good homes because they were themselves indigent.

Only after Amanda passed muster were the two of us allowed to enter the feline domicile area.

The big cages inside the area were also spotless, and the tile floors and walls had been newly washed down. I caught a faint whiff of Lysol in the air. There were several open pens on the window side, where the cats were allowed to gambol either singly or in pairs, depending on their disposition.

Three women volunteers in white-and-red-checked smocks ran the show. A list of commands was printed in bold block type on one wall:

A CAT OF ONE'S OWN

DO NOT PICK UP ANY CAT WITHOUT PERMISSION!
DO NOT PUT YOUR FINGERS INTO ANY CAGE!
YOU MUST WASH YOUR HANDS AFTER HANDLING ANY CAT!

A smiling volunteer approached us. Her name tag identified her as Sis Norlich. "Just take your time, ladies. Look around. It's a full house today. Everybody here needs a good home. And aren't they all lovely!"

Amanda and I started making our rounds, Miss Norlich following us closely, as if perhaps we were not to be trusted.

And what a beautiful melange of cats we saw. All shapes, colors, personalities. It was almost too sad to bear. If I had the room—say, a huge old house on a big piece of land with two barns—I would have taken them all.

I looked up to see Amanda pointing across the aisle.

There was a leg sticking far out of one of the cages. It was indeed a humorous sight. The cat attached to that leg was sleeping splayed out like a bear rug.

Amanda crossed the aisle and I followed her. The ever-watchful volunteer followed me.

We peered into the cage.

"Will you look at her!" Amanda exclaimed.

"Actually, it's a him," Miss Norlich corrected her.

Whatever it was, it was the strangest-looking feline I had ever laid eyes on. The coloring of this cat was utterly unique.

Lydia Adamson

"Black and tan," Amanda said in amazement. "Almost the same color as Good Girl."

I dropped my voice down to a whisper. "Did you by any chance tell the interviewer you have a dog at home?"

"No," she whispered back. "Why?"

"Sometimes cat people can be unyielding about canines. Better not say anything."

She nodded. "Have you ever seen a cat like this before?"

"Never," I said.

The small short-haired cat had a two-color coat, perfectly bifurcated from the tip of his rosy pink nose right down the middle of his back, perfectly symmetrical. Tan, almost rust, on the right side, black on the left.

Perfectly symmetrical: even down to the ears, one tan and one black.

It was as if someone had taken half of one cat and joined it with half of another. He was a perfect little harlequin.

His tail, however, was solid black, and had a tuft of brown at the very tip.

"That's Jake. You don't want him."

It was a woman who had spoken, another volunteer.

"Why not?" I asked, catching only part of her name tag: Jill.

"Jake's something of a problem," she answered crisply.

I stared at the sleeping harlequin. He didn't look like a problem to me. But if a shelter volunteer was warning us off him, I figured it was probably best to heed her advice.

Gently I pulled Amanda away from the cage and we resumed our walk around the room.

A black lady cat with a white face caught Amanda's eye, as did a frisky tortoiseshell, and then a very young tabby with big ears.

Each one was taken out of its cage by a volunteer and Amanda, after obeying the hand-washing ritual, was allowed to hold him or her briefly. She had never held a cat before in her life, and didn't know what to do once the parcel was placed in her arms. I could read the fear on her face as each kitty mewled or nuzzled her or struggled to get away.

"All three of the ones you held are winners," said volunteer Sis. "It's hard to choose, isn't it?"

Amanda didn't answer. Instead, she suddenly wheeled and pointed to the cage with the harlequin cat—Jake.

"Him!" she pronounced loudly. "I want him!"

We were immediately surrounded by the volunteers, including a third woman, Ollie Something-or-other.

It was she who counseled: "We see by your interview report that this is your first cat. Believe me, Jake isn't for you. He's quite a handful."

"What does he do?" I inquired.

"He's just . . . difficult . . . at times," she stuttered.

"I don't care," Amanda declared stubbornly. "I want Jake."

"Just a minute, Amanda," I said. "Maybe you ought to listen to them."

She gave me a dirty look, her face set in stone. "I've made up my mind, Alice. It's Jake."

I said nothing further.

"Very well," Sis Norlich said doubtfully. "Go into the Get Acquainted Room and we'll bring him in to you."

Amanda and I walked down the hall, and after washing her hands one last time she went alone into a small enclosed space, one wall of which was a window. A lone wooden chair was pulled up to a long, low table. The cat was delivered as promised.

I watched through the glass as Jake gave Amanda a lazy, appraising look, then promptly fell asleep again. Following his lead, she lay her head down close to his and closed her eyes.

Five minutes later one of the volunteers opened the door.

"We get along perfectly fine," said Amanda. "He's no problem at all."

Amanda took Jake out of the shelter in a new carrier. I toted the bag of litter, the litter box, and the two kinds of cat food that Abide offered at prices below those of the neighborhood supermarkets.

We quickly found a cab.

"Maybe I ought to go back with you," I told Amanda. "Just in case."

"Just in case what?" she snapped.

"You know . . . what with the dog and all."

"How many times must I tell you, Alice? Ivan told me Good Girl was raised with cats, that she gets along better with them than with other dogs."

"I understand that," I said, "but you might need some help lugging all this stuff."

"Oh." She then apologized for snapping at me and agreed to let me help.

The taxi ride was fine. Being in a carrier in a fast-moving vehicle didn't seem to faze Jake at all. In fact, he looked positively bored.

Once back in the apartment, with the carrier in the center of the living room, Amanda turned to me. "What do I do now?"

"Open it."

When she had done so, Jake stepped out, stretched, and began to survey his new home.

Good Girl, still on her rug, thumped her tail mightily in approval. Then she struggled to her feet and approached the cat.

Jake dropped low, belly on the carpet, his coat bristling. He began to hiss threateningly.

Good Girl stopped in her tracks, her feelings obviously hurt at Jake's out-and-out aggression. She walked back to her part of the room and lay down again.

I breathed easier. Then I showed Amanda how to set up the litter box and how much to feed the cat.

I was stunned when I noticed that Amanda was crying.

I rushed to her side. "What is it?"

"It's just that I realize the first wonderful thing I ever did for Ivan—I did after he died."

There wasn't much I could say.

In a minute she dried her eyes, thanked me for my assistance, and sent me away with three blueberry muffins.

That same evening, at home in my loft, I was recounting the events of the day to Tony Basillio, who had brought in a Turkish meal from a new takeout place on Bleecker Street.

He was eating as I talked. My two cats, Bushy and Pancho, were at our feet, trying to fake an interest in my story by sitting up attentively. Of course, what they were really doing was waiting to see if Tony would take pity on them and hand over some barbecued lamb.

When I finished the tale, Tony arched his thick eyebrows; the gesture only seemed to intensify his good looks. When he was younger, people said he should have been a soap opera heartthrob rather than a penurious stage designer.

"Sounds like everything ended well, Swede," he remarked. "The shelter placed the cat. This Jake found a cushy home for himself. Your friend Amanda made good on her dead husband's wish. The old dog has a new friend. And you did a good deed."

He chewed some, holding up his hand when I

attempted to speak, which meant that his analysis was not yet concluded.

"The only thing I don't get," he continued, "is the cat itself. I mean, I just can't believe there's an animal that's one color on one side and another color on the other side."

"Tony, believe me, it's true. Think of a harlequin—or, you know, the jester in an Elizabethan drama. They often wore those pink and white costumes, the colors split right down the middle of the body . . . and different-colored bells on each shoe."

The ringing phone interrupted us. It was Amanda calling. She was frantic, almost screaming into the receiver. "Jake's in an absolute frenzy, Alice! I swear he's going crazy. He's in the litter box, and he's kicking every bit of the—the whatsit?—that gravel—out of the pan. It's everywhere I look, Alice—everywhere! He's acting as if he's lost his—"

"Amanda!" I barked. "Shut up for a minute!"

I had shocked her into silence. I could hear her breathing heavily.

"Listen to me, Amanda. I want you to calm down. It's nothing, what you're describing. A lot of cats kick their litter about as though they're digging a tunnel. It means nothing. In fact, it's good news. It simply shows that Jake took to the litter box quickly."

She didn't speak for a long time. Then she said sheepishly, "I'm a fool, Alice. Forgive me."

"Forget it. Everything's going to be fine. You can always call me if anything happens."

She hung up then. I began to clean up Tony's Turkish mess while he gave me one of his merciless reviews of the sets in an Australian tap dance musical that he'd recently seen. I wasn't really listening. I'm an actress. Sets usually leave me cold. I prefer a bare stage, truth be told, and a good script—and an audience, of course.

The telephone rang again. Amanda again. But this time she didn't sound hysterical, only worried.

"There's trouble, Alice."

"What trouble?"

"With Jake. He won't eat. Anything. I put out a bowl of dry food, like you told me, and a plate of that turkey in savory juices, and a bowl of water—just like you said. He walked over, sniffed at all of it, and walked away. So I tried giving him a dish of cream. No good. Even cottage cheese with peaches. He just won't touch any of it, Alice. He's going to starve if he goes on like this. And to make it worse, Good Girl is eating his food now. But he doesn't care at all! What am I going to do?"

"Amanda, it's nothing to get worked up about. Just stop worrying."

"How can I stop worrying? He'll starve!"

"Look, Jake's in a strange place, a new home. He may not eat until he feels comfortable. You have to remember, Jake isn't Good Girl. He may eat on schedule; he may not. He may eat only the dry food or only the canned, or both.

You just can't predict what a cat will eat and when. They're finicky gourmands. Just put the food out and give him plenty of fresh water . . . and then forget about it. Look at my Pancho. There's only one thing he'd exert himself for, and that's saffron rice. You figure it out."

That crisis defused, Amanda rang off again.

Basillio was on the floor now, playing his game with Pancho, whom Tony fondly referred to as "the psychopath," because Panch spent most of his time fleeing or scheming against imaginary enemies.

The game was simple. Tony would meow, snarl, moan, growl, and make all manner of weird noises. Then, pretending to be Peter Lorre, he would inform Panch that no matter how long it took, he was going to "get him on some dark night and hang him high from a church steeple for his crimes against the feline nation."

Pancho, whom none of us would ever truly understand, seemed to find Tony's threats soothing. He sat about ten feet away from the sprawled-out Basillio and looked upon him benignly.

Again the phone rang.

"Is that chick crazy?" Tony shouted. "It's only a cat!"

"Maybe it isn't Amanda this time," I suggested with a sigh.

Oh, but it was. Her voice, however, was far from hysteria. In fact, it was hushed and full of amazement.

"You won't believe what's happening now," she said, barely audible.

"Try me."

"I'm looking at Jake right now. Do you know where he is?"

"No."

"At the very top of the window. On *top* of the shutter."

"So?"

Her voice seemed to grow more and more desperate.

"How am I going to get him down from there, Alice? What if he falls? What'll I do?"

"Don't do anything. Cats climb. Cats jump. They get very high up sometimes. It looks scarier to us than it does to them. But believe me, he won't fall. He'll be okay, Amanda. He probably likes it up there. Maybe he wanted a deluxe river view."

I heard her short, disbelieving laugh.

"Take it easy, Amanda. Read a book. Listen to the radio or something. It might even be a good idea to get out of the house altogether. Why don't you go for a nice walk. Just forget about him for a while."

"I don't know, I don't know," she replied softly. "He's just so . . . high up there. And the top of the shutter is so narrow. I'd hate to think of what—"

"Hey, Amanda. You ought to take a sleeping pill and go to bed," I said sternly.

To my surprise, she agreed. "Yes," she said, "I think that might be best."

Amanda hung up then. Tony looked worriedly at me. "We'd better get out of here, Nestleton. This Amanda is going to be calling all night. She's even worse than I was when you foisted those two Siamese on me last Christmas. Let Bushy answer the phone. Seems to me he's the one who'd know what to advise her about this Jake."

"What are you suggesting, Tony?"

"My apartment or a movie."

"A movie it is."

There were no further calls from Amanda for the next few days. On Sunday morning I slipped into a rather chic fall outfit, preparatory to meeting Tony. We would then proceed across town to the theater district, where my friend Nora ran a special little restaurant called the Pal Joey Bistro. Nora had only recently decided to start serving Sunday brunch, and Basillio and I had been invited for inaugural eggs Benedict and mimosas.

Just as I was leaving—and I do mean *just*—I was blowing a good-bye kiss to the cats while fishing keys from my purse—the telephone rang. Thinking it might be Tony, I picked up.

Alas, Amanda's whiskey-thick voice greeted me. All she said was, "Alice. He's gone."

"Gone? Who's gone?"

"Jake."

"What do you mean, Amanda?" I asked, trying not to sound annoyed.

"Just what I said. He vanished. When I got up this morning he was gone."

"Did you leave any of the windows or doors open?"

"No!"

"Then he isn't 'gone,' Amanda. He's only hiding. He's probably sleeping in a closet or behind a desk somewhere."

"No, he isn't. I checked. I've looked everywhere for him." Her voice had become tremulous.

"Don't be silly, Amanda. Cats can find all kinds of strange places to hide. He'll come out as soon as he gets hungry."

The dam broke then. She was crying inconsolably, muttering incoherently about her late husband; how her life had gone wrong and would never be good again.

I realized I'd better get over there.

"Just hang on, Amanda. Wait for me. I'll come and find Jake for you."

I called Tony and told him I'd meet him at Pal Joey, asking him to apologize to Nora for me because I'd be a little late.

Then I rushed out, hopped a cab, and sped to Amanda's place.

The man who answered her door was about forty, very thin, with a bushy mane of reddish hair. He was wearing a gray gym outfit.

"I'm a friend of Amanda's," he said in answer to my unspoken question. "Harvey Stith. I live just up the block. She called me. Sounded as if she was cracking up."

Harvey Stith! "*The* Harvey Stith?" I asked, shaking his proffered hand awkwardly.

"Well, I suppose so. I didn't think anyone remembered my name," he said shyly and chuckled.

He was wrong—I remembered his name. Stith had been one of those meteoric *wunderkinds* who exploded onto Broadway in the early 1980s. Singer, dancer, song writer, director—you name it, he did it.

But then the bubble burst. I heard he had forsaken the commercial theater and accepted a position as director of one of those ambitious graduate programs in theater arts at a California university.

He ushered me in. Poor Amanda, the phone still in her lap, was on the rug beside Good Girl. Two more sorrowful creatures I had never seen.

I looked around the apartment, more critically this time. It had many nooks and crannies, many bookcases and shelves and cabinets and obviously many closets. Jake could be anywhere.

"Stay where you are, Amanda," I told her. "Harvey and I will find him. All you have to do is tell us which closets have trunks or cartons or hat boxes without a lid—that kind of stuff."

She pointed to the hallway.

"Jake-O!" I called. "Come out come out wherever you are." I then commenced my search, opening the closet door. Inside were enough boxes for a flock of shy cats to hide in for a week.

Even with my head inside the closet, I could hear the telephone ring. I wondered if Amanda had made hysterical phone calls to everyone she knew, asking for their help in finding the cat. "Jake-O!" I continued to call. "You come out here this minute!"

It wasn't the cat whose shrill cry I heard. It was Amanda's—she was screaming into the receiver: "But how . . . *How?!* The banks are closed today!"

I walked quickly back to the living room and again looked to Harvey Stith for an answer. He only shrugged.

Amanda hung up abruptly.

She was on her feet by then, shaking, her face bloodless. "He said he has Jake," she announced in a monotone. "He said he wants fifteen thousand dollars or I'll never see Jake again. He said he'd call back in twenty minutes."

"Is this some kind of joke, Amanda?" I asked.

She didn't answer. She knelt beside Good Girl and pulled at one of her ears.

"Something tells me it isn't a joke," Harvey Stith said.

"This man who called," I said, "do you know him, Amanda?"

She shook her head vehemently.

"Are you sure that's what he said? That he wanted fifteen thousand dollars for Jake."

"Fifteen thousand," she repeated. "If I want him back. He'll call again in twenty minutes." And she began to giggle.

Oh, Lord, I thought, she's going to lose control altogether. Harvey and I got her up and led her to a chair. She was tense as a trip wire, fighting panic.

"How could this person have gotten Jake?" she whispered. "How did he get in? When?"

"Call the police, Amanda," Harvey urged.

"No! No police! I want Jake back!"

"But this is insane. Fifteen thousand? You can't just give this man fifteen thousand dollars for an animal you've had for only a few days—a stray from a shelter."

Amanda looked up at me beseechingly. "What would you do, Alice?"

I couldn't answer. I didn't have fifteen thousand dollars. If someone kidnapped one of my cats and demanded a ransom for his safe return, I'd pay anything. But it wasn't for me to say what Amanda should do. The whole thing was so strange. More than just strange, it was unreal.

"Call the police, Amanda," Stith said again. "This is serious business."

"I said no!"

Harvey looked to me for support. But I steadfastly refused to intervene. There were conflicting theories about bringing the police in on kidnappings. Sometimes it worked out for the best; sometimes it ended in tragedy.

We waited in eerie silence.

The apartment became oppressive, as if it were sucking the air out of our lungs. Oddly enough, I could sense the presence of that harlequin cat.

The follow-up call came. Amanda picked up the receiver slowly and brought it to her ear. "Yes . . . yes," she murmured, and then she fell silent, listening. She did not look at Harvey or me.

At last she hung up.

"All right. It's set," she told us.

"What's set?" asked Harvey.

"I will go to the bank tomorrow and get the fifteen thousand in twenties and fifties. I'll bring the money to Forty-sixth Street and Twelfth Avenue tomorrow night at ten-thirty. He'll turn Jake over to me and I'll give him the money. I must come alone."

An expression of utter disgust crossed Harvey's face. "This is stupid and dangerous."

"Amanda," I said, "that is a very desolate area at night."

"I don't care. Will you help me—both of you?"

"How?" I asked.

"Just stay close. A block or two away. Then come and collect me and Jake. I know I'll be exhausted and frightened. I won't make it back home by myself."

What choice did we have? Harvey Stith and I made our arrangements: Meet at 10:00 P.M. at the luncheonette on Fifty-seventh Street at Eleventh Avenue. Then go and collect Amanda and, we hoped, Jake.

I went on to brunch at the restaurant. I didn't say a word about what was going on to Nora and Tony. It was too difficult to explain—too—well, as I said, unreal.

A CAT OF ONE'S OWN

*   *   *

I spent Monday in a fog of anxiety and indecision. For hours at a time I contemplated the possibility that someone might someday kidnap my own cats.

Several times I felt the urge to phone Amanda and tell her that Harvey Stith was right: the police should be brought in. But I never made that call. Few things in my life I regret more than not making that call.

At nine that evening I took a bus uptown. Harvey was already at the luncheonette when I arrived. We sat glumly in the booth with ripped leather, drinking coffee, not talking at all.

There seemed to be nothing to say. Nothing about our common interest in the theater; nothing about each other's personal life; nothing about Amanda; nothing about Jake the cat, the unfortunate kidnap victim; not even a banal exchange about the weather.

At twenty minutes past ten we began walking toward Twelfth Avenue. The sky was like black velvet—that's how dark it was—and the wind off the water was cutting.

On the avenue now, we turned south, heading for Forty-sixth Street, where Amanda was to meet the kidnapper.

The piers loomed up on our right. Not a living soul on the street. The only lights came from the truck traffic on the avenue.

At Fiftieth Street, Harvey stopped and squinted at his watch. "We'd better hurry. The exchange should be happening about now," he said.

We picked up our pace, fighting the wind.

Forty-ninth. Forty-eighth. Forty-seventh. No more words exchanged.

"I think I can see her!" he burst out suddenly. "Yes, I see her!"

"Where?" I asked excitedly as we began to run.

"Up ahead, Alice. There! Thank God, she's all right."

Amen, I thought, seeing Amanda for myself then. She was leaning against a No Parking post, waiting for us. And Jake was all right too, snuggled up against her.

Amanda must have seen us at just about the same moment, because she seemed to be smiling at us. She was waving to us with one hand and holding tightly to Jake with the other.

Smiling, I said. But that wasn't true.

I was mistaken. That was no smile.

Amanda fell forward, and in that second, Jake leapt clear.

Harvey caught her. The dead weight of her body spun him around and they both went sprawling to the pavement.

Then and only then did I see the ice pick in Amanda's back.

Chapter 2

Seven and a half hours after we found Amanda with Jake in her arms and an ice pick in her back . . . six o'clock in the morning . . . four people were in Amanda's Beekman Place apartment.

I sat next to the two homicide detectives, Yvonne Webster and Art Luboff.

Harvey Stith was standing with the telephone in hand. He was trying to reach Amanda's sister Gloria in Beloit, Wisconsin.

His conversation with the long-distance information source was loud and brusque, but the moment he made contact with the sister, his voice dropped to a near-whisper and he turned away from us. We could hear nothing.

There were muffled words. Then silence. Then more

muffled words. We knew what he was telling her, though—that Amanda had been murdered.

Finally, his hand cupped over the speaker, he faced us again.

"She wants to speak to you, Alice," Harvey said.

"Me? Why?" I didn't know Amanda's sister and had no desire to speak to her. I was oh so weary.

"She says she has heard of you," he answered. "She's a bit dazed. I woke her and I don't know if she understands exactly what's happened."

"What did you tell her?"

"The essentials."

Yvonne Webster, the short, heavyset black woman detective, was staring at me censoriously. She was put out, presumably, by my hesitation to take the phone. The other detective was looking at the strange duo on the floor: Jake and Good Girl.

The cat was napping on his back. The Gordon setter sat close to him, her tail thumping contentedly.

I took the phone and identified myself to Gloria Avery. Her voice kept cracking into different registers. She wanted me to stay on in Amanda's apartment until she arrived. She wanted me to look after Good Girl and the new cat. She would come to New York very quickly, she said. There would be a lot of work to do, many details to be seen to. The estate of a husband and wife who died within a few months of each other would be a complex matter.

After she added, "Amanda was so fond of you," she broke down completely.

A few minutes later I hung up.

Harvey Stith gave me an extremely nervous look. I knew what it was about. Why were the detectives still hovering? It had been such a long night. First, the wait for the police and ambulance. Then the ride to the hospital, where Amanda was confirmed DOA. Next, the station house, where the police had requested our fingerprints—though it turned out there were no recognizable prints on the ice pick to match up.

Finally, back to Amanda's row house apartment, where the detectives had conducted a quiet but thorough search. And here they remained, still hovering.

Detective Webster, who was wearing a green turtleneck, finally got to the point. "We've got a few problems here," she said.

"To say the least," seconded Detective Luboff.

"Problem number one," Detective Webster said, "the call."

"Call?" I asked. "What call?"

Her voice was accusatory. "The call none of you ever made—to the police. To report the . . . uh . . . kidnapping."

"Amanda wanted the cat back," said Harvey. "That's all she wanted. I urged her to phone the police, but she wouldn't do it."

Detective Webster ignored him. "And we got a problem about that cat," she noted.

"What problem is that?" I asked dutifully.

"He vanishes from the apartment. There was no break-in. Only three people have access to the place: you two and Amanda Avery herself."

There seemed to be no answer to that point.

"And we've got a third problem," she went on. "In these kinds of deals, if the meet comes off, if the payoff happens, usually it's smooth sailing. No violence. But this time the vic winds up with an ice pick in her back after the money has changed hands, and *after* the cat has been returned. It makes no sense."

"No sense at all," seconded Luboff.

"Unless Avery identified the kidnapper," the female detective added. "Unless she recognized him—knew him."

She looked at me, hard, then over at Harvey. "But you two are alibied up, right? By each other. Isn't that the case? Neither of you was at the scene. You were just tagging along, trailing at a distance. Isn't that true?" I hated the tone of her voice. When neither Harvey nor I responded to the obviously rhetorical questions she had posed, she added, "Odd, don't you think? Damn odd. And damn convenient."

Without further word, she stood to leave. Detective Luboff got to his feet as well. He pointed to Jake. "Fifteen thousand is a helluva lot of cash for that stupid-looking cat."

The two detectives left then.

Five minutes later, Harvey left. We did not exchange a word other than "good night."

I lay down wearily on the rug not far from Jake and Good Girl and fell fast asleep, fully clothed.

Chapter 3

I dreamt I was drowning. I awoke with a start. But it was no ocean wave lapping at me; it was Good Girl's tongue.

It was about ten a.m. I'd slept only three hours. I undressed, showered, found some old things of Amanda's in the bedroom closet, and changed into them. Then I took Good Girl out for a walk. When I returned I fed her and Jake, who seemed sublimely bored by everything.

Then and only then did I call Tony to ask him to get over to my loft and feed Bushy and Pancho.

"Where are you?" Tony asked, the mistrust heavy in his voice. He suspected another man, obviously.

I not only told him where I was but why—the whole messy thing.

"I can't leave you alone for five minutes," he said.

When Harvey Stith came back to the apartment around 11:30, he was in the company of a woman who had known Amanda. Joan Engel was a theatrical producer. I liked her immediately. She was older than I, dressed chicly but not ostentatiously, and spoke in the nervous, nitty-gritty, rapid-fire style that characterizes so many people at the business end of show business. Her language was earthy, cryptic, and invigorating.

She said of poor Jake the cat: "With a coat like that, I couldn't even book him in Bosnia."

I made coffee. We talked about Amanda for twenty minutes, reminiscing. Of course they had known her better than I . . . but not longer.

When they left, I went back to bed. In the late afternoon I took a walk, ate in a Chinese restaurant on First Avenue, and returned to Amanda's place around five.

In front of the house, waiting for me, stood a younger, plainer, taller version of Amanda Avery. It should have been obvious immediately, but it took me a while to realize that this had to be Amanda's sister.

She spoke before I had the chance to. "You must be the actress," she said.

"Yes. Alice Nestleton."

"I just arrived. I checked into the Beekman Hotel, around the corner. Expensive! It's ridiculously expensive, in fact."

I opened the door and held it for her. But Gloria Avery

seemed reluctant to go into the apartment. She stood in the open doorway taking deep breaths, as though some unseen force were constricting her breathing.

"Is that *the* cat?" she asked when we were at last inside.

I looked over at Jake. "Yes."

"How? Why . . . ?" she began to shout, but soon dissolved into tears. Both Jake and Good Girl edged away from us.

Gloria tugged at my coatsleeve. "I don't understand. Do you understand it? I mean, why did she die for that thing? Why didn't she let them have it? That stupid animal doesn't even know what he caused. Look at him!"

She was circling the room in a fury, alternately weeping and cursing Jake. Finally she collapsed against the closet door.

All I could say in Jake's defense was, "Your sister thought she was fulfilling a promise to her dying husband."

"You mean Ivan Tasso—that idiot? Pardon me for speaking ill of the dead. I only met him once. But believe me, Amanda's loyalty to him was inexplicable. I didn't have the least idea what she saw in him. Sure, he was well off, but it wasn't the money. Amanda was never interested in money."

Gloria Avery looked around suddenly, intently. "I've never been in this apartment before. I hate it."

After that outburst, she seemed to settle down. She walked to a chair and sat down primly upon it.

"Can I get you something, Gloria? Maybe a cup of coffee?"

"No. I had better start looking for her manuscripts. That's what my sister would have wanted me to do. They were the only things that really mattered to her."

She stood. "You're very kind to help me out, Alice. Please forgive my hysteria. I know I'm not acting very well."

"It's understandable."

She went through the place like a tornado. But Gloria did not find what she was looking for. She rested for a while and then started the search again.

A while later I heard her cry out from the kitchen.

"Look! Look!" she implored when I ran in.

On the refrigerator door, which seemed to have functioned as a bulletin board for Amanda, a banana-shaped magnet held up a copy of a contract with a storage warehouse on Varick Street, along with a small piece of paper containing a series of handwritten numbers. The address was not far from my place.

"She must have put the papers into storage for safekeeping," Gloria reasoned. "And the numbers on this paper must be the combination to a locker or something like that."

"Maybe," I conceded. "But why would she do that? She was continually working on her study of Virginia Woolf, wasn't she?"

"Yes. But if the manuscript's not in the apartment, it has to be here." She tapped the paper emphatically.

"Maybe," I repeated.

"And her files," Gloria added. "Where are they? Amanda read and saved every critical article ever written on Woolf—in about ten languages. If her files aren't in the apartment, they have to be in this storage room as well."

I shrugged.

"I want to go there. Now. Will you take me, Alice? I don't know New York at all."

"It might not be open at this time," I said.

"Yes it is," she insisted. "See? It says here: twenty-four-hour access."

So, armed with two large empty shopping bags, we found a cab and took it downtown.

I had heard of these mini-storage warehouses but never used or visited one before. This one was like an old-fashioned penitentiary. Floor upon floor with hundreds of locked rooms on each—like cells, except they had no bars. Each bin was identical, the size of a very small hotel room. The walls, floors, and doors of the bins seemed to be aluminum siding. I wondered if anyone had ever slept in one.

It took us ten fumbling minutes to execute the combination on the lock. Then we were inside.

Gloria's face lit up like a candle. All of Amanda's precious papers were there—files, notes, manuscripts, computer discs.

"I don't understand why she kept the material here," I said. "It's as if she had suspended work on her projects. That's unlike your sister."

"Maybe she worked here."

"I doubt that. Look at this place. Cramped. Dark. No water or air. Not even a toilet."

"I suppose you're right," Gloria noted. "But it doesn't matter now," she added sadly.

Handling every scrap with great reverence, she began packing the papers and discs pertaining to her sister's perpetually expanding and never finished critical thesis on Virginia Woolf, and the one-woman play based on Woolf's fascinating diaries—similarly unfinished. The files she left untouched.

We took one last look around and prepared to leave. But then Gloria stopped in her tracks, suddenly dropping the full shopping bags on the floor. Tears streamed down her face.

"What does all her work mean now? Nothing. Soon it'll be dust—like her. All those years! All that work! And she gets herself killed in an instant—over a stupid cat! An animal she had just taken into her home. Oh, God!"

There seemed little that I could say, so I didn't try. I bent to help her with the shopping bags.

"No!" she said sharply. "I'll carry them. She was *my* sister."

Then she pointed to the corner of the room and said, crazily, "You take that! Or the mice will get it."

I saw the large cookie tin—five-pound capacity—she was pointing at. It was a brand of French butter cookie I recognized, and the less said about my familiarity with it, the better. I walked over, picked up the tin, and opened the lid with some difficulty. There were no cookies inside. I shook the contents out onto the floor.

The first thing to drop out was a much-handled old paperback copy of the Virginia Woolf novel *Mrs. Dalloway.*

Then came newspaper clippings . . . dozens of them. All theater reviews from the past few years. Most of them cut out of New York City newspapers.

Gloria and I looked at each other blankly.

"Leave it," she finally said. "Just leave it all there."

Leave it? A beautiful tin like that? I have always loved empty tins. Tea bag tins. Cookie tins. Hard candy tins. I keep all sorts of odds and ends in them, from subway tokens and loose change to laundry tickets to earrings to thumb-tacks. So I hastily put back the book and the clippings, fastened the lid, and put the tin into one of the shopping bags.

When the cab dropped us back at Amanda's, Detectives Webster and Luboff were waiting for us in that long, mean-looking car of theirs.

"Why don't you go on inside, Miss Nestleton," Detective Webster suggested, speaking through a rolled-down window. "We want to talk to Amanda Avery's sister alone."

And give her pneumonia by keeping her out here in the freezing air, I thought. The night was cold, dark, and windy. But I didn't protest. I followed the "suggestion" and went in.

Good Girl seemed to have become morose. Maybe she

had finally realized that she had now lost Amanda as well as Ivan Tasso. Maybe she realized that she had outlived them both.

As for Jake the cat, he was balanced up on top of the shutters, looking out at the dark night. I remembered that his being up there had scared Amanda silly. I wasn't worried about him, really, but it was a very narrow, high ledge.

Jake began to stare at me, his ears pulling forward. I stared back at him. He yawned, licked his right front paw for a bit, sighed, and then turned his gaze back to me.

What an odd cat he was. So cool, so controlled. Jake had been taken from his original home and dumped into a shelter; then adopted by a woman who knew absolutely nothing about cats; then kidnapped; then made to witness a grisly murder. Yet he appeared unscathed, unconcerned, unaffected.

The room's light and shadow played on his strange bifurcated coat. He looked otherworldly. I felt a chill and took a step backward. Was it possible that this kitty frightened me?

Gloria Avery came in just then.

"What did they want?" I asked.

"Nothing much. First they explained the status of the investigation, which is more or less nowhere. They're canvassing the neighborhood to see if any dog walkers might have seen anything. Then they asked me questions about Amanda's private life, of which I knew nothing except that she was a widow. Oh, by the way, they want to talk to you now."

I made a disgusted sound way back in my throat and put my coat back on. When the two police detectives saw me on the sidewalk, they motioned that I should climb into the back seat of the car. The female detective, Webster, did most of the talking, but she didn't turn around to look at me. Instead she watched me through the rearview mirror.

"You live alone, Miss Nestleton?" she asked.

"No. I live with two cats."

"But you have a man friend."

I laughed at the phrase before answering. "Yes, I do."

"His name?"

"Anthony Basillio."

"Occupation?"

"Stage designer, when he works."

"Does he stay over at your place?"

"Sometimes."

"We'd like to be able to contact him."

I was beginning to bristle at her prying, but I knew better than to ask why she wanted to contact Tony. I gave his address and phone number. The other detective wrote down the information.

"We know where the calls demanding the money came from," Detective Webster informed me.

"Where?"

"A pay phone on Carmine Street," she said.

"Oh?"

"That's near your apartment, isn't it, Miss Nestleton?"

"Pretty near," I said. It didn't take a genius to figure out where this was leading. "Surely," I said, "you can't think I made those calls. I was in Amanda's apartment when she received the first call. I was helping her look for the cat."

"Yes, but where was this Basillio?"

"I know where he was supposed to be: waiting for me at a restaurant. But why don't you ask him yourself!" I said sharply.

"We're going to. Thank you for your time, Miss Nestleton."

I slammed the car door shut behind me and walked briskly back to the house.

Gloria had not yet removed her outer garments. She was seated on a plush chair, the shopping bags beside her. Good Girl's trusting face rested on Gloria's knee and Jake, back on level ground now, crouched nearby, watching the two of them.

"Please, Alice," said Gloria, pointing to a facing chair, "sit down."

I did so. Her voice sounded very peculiar.

"I can't stay here, Alice. I just don't want to be in this apartment. I don't want to be in New York. I just want to take my sister's body home."

"But you have things to take care of, Gloria. You must—"

"No! No! The first thing in the morning, I'll call my

lawyer in Beloit and he'll give me the name of a New York lawyer. I don't care about the fees. Let him have the whole damn estate, as long as he can take care of everything and keep me out of it. I just want to get out of here and take Amanda home."

She looked over at Jake as if he were evil incarnate.

"I hope," she said after a minute, "you will adopt them."

"What? You mean Jake . . . and Good Girl?"

"Yes."

"I'm sorry, Gloria. I can't. I have two cats at home."

"Then please put them up for adoption, if that's how it works. Find homes for them, that's what I mean."

"Why don't you take them?" I said.

"Absolutely not."

"Listen, Gloria. Good Girl is an old dog. And Jake here is . . . strange-looking. I think it would be very difficult to find new homes for them."

"Then do something else with them! Anything!" she shouted. "I don't care. Have them put down."

"I can't do that," I said quietly. "I won't."

"You have to help me on this, Alice. You're the only person I know here. Amanda was your friend. I have to get out of here . . . Please!"

Oh, what a mess I've gotten myself into, I thought. It was bad enough being party to the gruesome murder of a friend—albeit an unwitting party. But that paled before my fear and loathing at the thought of abandoning these creatures.

I closed my eyes and tried to think of a way out. There wasn't one. When I opened them again, I saw that Gloria was crying, Good Girl was sleeping, and Jake was calmly helping himself to the dog's food.

Chapter 4

Gloria packed up and went home the next morning, as promised. I was left to arrange the adoptions of Good Girl and Jake. I divided my time between my downtown loft and Amanda's Beekman Place home, which meant I was feeding and caring for three cats and one canine senior citizen.

During the next few days I made more than a hundred calls. I phoned every person for whom I had ever done cat-sitting work. I called acquaintances from the theater world and forced them to call their acquaintances. I contacted the various people I'd met over the years who worked with animal rescue groups. I pestered Harvey Stith. I even collared strangers on the street.

And, in desperation, I called Sam Tully. Now, that was an experience.

"How ya been, honey?" asked the old mystery writer/derelict . . . the creator of the hard-boiled detective Harry Bondo, who was now (happily, in my opinion) out of print.

I knew Sam still had his cat Pickles, but I thought there might be a chance he would take in Good Girl too.

"Listen, Nestleton, I got troubles. I can't handle any more."

"What kind of trouble, Tully?"

"They want me to write another Bondo mystery."

"That's trouble?"

"Wait. Listen. They want a Harry Bondo book without—get this, Nestleton—without sex, violence, or obscenity. Would you believe it?"

"I see why that would be trouble, Sam."

Then I told him about the catnapping and murder. After all, he was the man who had helped me get to the bottom of the Mary Singer murder. I also voiced my fear that I wouldn't be able to place Jake and Good Girl in proper homes.

"Guess we both got troubles, honey," he said. But that was as far as Tully's sympathies went; I could not convince him to adopt Good Girl.

I was panicking. What was I going to do with those two soon-to-be-homeless animals? Sure, there were shelters, like the one Jake had come from. But sooner or later every shelter had to put some of the animals down. Sooner or later.

I was not about to commit either of them to even the possibility of premature extinction.

What was going to happen to Amanda's apartment and everything in it? I really didn't know. I had to hope that one or the other of Gloria's attorneys would take care of that.

As for Amanda's friends Harvey Stith and Joan Engel— they had pulled a disappearing act. Neither of them had called or shown up again.

Even the two detectives had gone underground. They fell out of sight and out of touch after they'd questioned Tony.

Ten days after the murder, sprawled out on Amanda's sofa at ten o'clock in the evening, conversing with Jake and Good Girl in my fashion, I spotted that damn French cookie tin again.

I had forgotten all about it and it had remained where I'd placed it after returning from the storage bins: under the end table.

The thought came to me that if I retrieved it and opened it, I could spend some pleasant hours with Mrs. Dalloway.

This was a novel I had always loved, and so many years had passed since I last read it. Now it would be even more enjoyable. Being a good actress, I know that the second time around is always better than the first . . . and the third time can be ecstatic.

So I took the small paperback out of the tin, made

myself a cup of heady wild cherry tea, sat down, and began to read.

I was immediately engrossed in the story. *Mrs. Dalloway* is a novel about a mature upper-class English woman who is planning a party. The plot centers around an old flame of hers who returns from India and who may or may not attend that party. Complicating the plot is a young couple from a different social strata. They are deep in poverty, despair, and incipient psychosis. This couple, unintentionally, begins to interact with members of Clarissa Dalloway's circle.

It is a grand, complex, brilliantly written work, set in London between the two world wars. When I first read it, as a young woman, I was completely transported by the language and the interweaving of characters. Breathless with excitement, I couldn't imagine ever reading anything to match it.

Now, I was a little calmer.

But as I read I began to get irritated by the incessant underlining and notes in the margin.

I turned back to the front cover and saw the little red paste-on 49¢ tag. Amanda had obviously purchased it from the outdoor bins at the Strand, the well-known used bookstore on Broadway and 12th Street.

Who knew how many people had owned it before it showed up at the Strand, but obviously at one time it belonged to a student taking a course on the English novel.

I went back to reading. Then I realized that the notes were in Amanda's handwriting. I recognized her tiny, elegant script. But it seemed quite unlike her to have marked up a book, out of character somehow.

Something else was very strange, something about the markings themselves. They were purposeful in a peculiar way . . . not the way a student underlines an assigned text and not the way a teacher marks the text for a lecture.

If these were Amanda's notes—and I was sure they were—what were they about? I had one clue. Early on in the book, Clarissa Dalloway is in her fashionable townhouse coordinating her servants' efforts for the coming party. She hears a cook whistling in the kitchen and has a sense that all is right with the world.

Amanda had written in the margin: *What tune?*

I chewed on that for a while. It was telling me something.

Suddenly I realized what Amanda had been doing. A directorial read!

She was blocking out the text . . . pointing out incongruities . . . fleshing out characters . . . suggesting sets.

She had been reading the novel with a view toward staging it.

Very strange. Amanda Avery wasn't a theater person. She was an academic, an intellectual. Yes, she had been working on a one-woman play using Virginia Woolf's diaries—for years. But that was, frankly, an amateurish effort that even she seemed to realize would never be finished.

This annotation of *Mrs. Dalloway*, however, was very close to professional-level work by a director.

I put the book down. I remembered that along with the book in the cookie tin were dozens of theater reviews clipped from the New York papers. Why? Amanda used to make fun of the writing styles of people who reviewed movies and plays in the media.

I went over to her desk and found some samples of her handwriting. Yes, I had been correct, the annotations in the novel had been in Amanda's hand, beyond all doubt.

I picked up the phone and dialed Harvey Stith's number.

He answered right away. I could hear music in the background, and people talking.

"Good evening, Harvey. This is Alice Nestleton."

"Yes," he said, "I know."

"Are you available, Harvey? For a few minutes?"

"I have some people over."

He lived only two blocks away, so I was relentless. "It's important, Harvey. Just come by for a short while. I have to show you something."

I was waiting by the door when he entered.

Harvey sat down wearily and looked at the animals. "Any luck?" he asked.

"Not yet."

I handed him the paperback *Mrs. Dalloway*.

"What are you giving this to me for?"

"It was Amanda's copy," I said. "Did you ever see it before?"

He shook his head. "No."

"Leaf through it."

He did so.

"Do you see what she was doing, Harvey? She was blocking out passages. She was defining the characters—trying to adapt it to the stage."

He laughed abruptly. "Well, I don't know that I'd go that far. Amanda was a Woolf acolyte, but she never said anything to me about adapting any novel for the stage. There were those Woolf diaries, of course. She'd been working on those for ages. But no one took that too seriously. No, I never heard her mention *Mrs. Dalloway*. And I never saw this in her possession, either."

"All right," I said. "I want you to look at something else." I went for the cookie tin and the clippings, which I rather impolitely dumped into his lap.

"What are these?"

"Reviews of all kinds of plays and musical events. She must've clipped them out of newspapers."

"Really? Why?"

"I thought maybe you could tell me."

"I have no idea." Harvey seemed to be fascinated by the tin rather than the clippings. He was turning it slowly in his hands, studying the design.

His lack of interest in the reviews had deflected my expectations that *Mrs. Dalloway* was significant in some way to the murder of Amanda. "Thanks for coming over, Harvey."

"Why don't you come back with me for a drink."

"No, I have to get downtown."

He left then. I played with Good Girl for a while, scratching her stomach while she uttered mock growls.

Jake was prowling about the apartment, keeping an eye on us. He moved with great deliberation, placing each paw daintily, soundlessly onto the floor, almost in a hunting mode.

It was time to go. I shifted into my caretaker mode, making sure the animals' food and water bowls were filled and the litter box clean. Then I took Good Girl out for a brief walk.

But I didn't leave after the walk was over and the dog was back at home on her favorite pillow. I stood in the living room in my coat and pondered the ambiguities, if you'll pardon the expression.

There was a lot to ponder. First of all, the fact that while I was witness to virtually all the events leading up to the murder, I had never really believed the catnapping scenario.

Then I began to ponder the word *cliché*.

An acting teacher once told me, "Alice, you try too hard to be original. Deal with the clichés. They're usually true."

I knew a few clichés. For instance, "Out-of-work

actresses end up as either housewives, cat-sitters, or ladies of the night" (to use Sam Tully's archaic phrase).

Another one was, "Never speak ill of the dead."

And then there was, "Everyone leads at least two lives, and at least one of them is hidden."

And then . . . I was stumped. For the life of me, I couldn't come up with an ice pick cliché.

It was the "living two lives," etc., cliché that had riveted my attention.

How many lives had Amanda lived before she was murdered?

I now knew of at least three:

1. The austere reclusive Virginia Woolf scholar.

2. The devoted wife of an older, wealthy man who was gently obsessed with a Gordon setter bitch.

3. The avid theater follower who staged brilliant adaptations of great works of literature—but perhaps only in her head, in a fantasy world she had created.

I flicked on the light switch. My charges stared at me as I walked over to the desk and began to inspect the numerous small photos in leather frames there.

One of them was fairly recent—Amanda and, I suspected, Ivan Tasso, standing arm in arm in front of her place near Northampton. I recognized the charming little house, having visited her there a couple of times.

I closed the small wallet-like leather frame containing the snapshot and slipped it into my pocket. Then I shut the light off, cautioning Jake and Good Girl against any bad behavior, and left.

It was time to assemble my company of players.

The following day, just before the noon hour, I entered the Pal Joey Bistro in the theater district. My friend Nora Karroll, owner, manager, hostess, and sometime chef of said bistro, sat fuming in her small, cluttered office near the kitchen.

On the walls were photographs of her when she was a musical comedy actress. Nora could sing and dance up a storm. She was never a Broadway luminary, but an *almost* luminary—a perpetual second lead who consistently garnered good reviews but never broke through to stardom. Of course, by the time I met her, her high-kicking days were over. She was one of the older students in the very serious acting class where Tony Basillio and I first met. Like most of us in the business, she had a second life now, as a successful restaurateur.

Also featured on the wall were photos of her with several celebrities from the theater world who occasionally drank themselves into a stupor at Pal Joey's. There was even a picture of an ex-governor of New York having a grand time at the bistro, wearing a New Year's Eve party hat and staring at Nora's décolletage. At age fifty-whatever, Nora was still a looker, as my friend Sam Tully would say.

"Sit down, Alice. You won't believe what happened to me this morning!"

I dutifully swiped papers off the chair and took a seat.

"Just listen to this," Nora went on. "I brought some clothes into this posh dry cleaner this morning, on my way to work. So I give them the stuff, they give me a ticket—the usual—and I walk out. Okay? Once I'm outside, I take a few steps and I get the feeling that I forgot to take the ticket. So I head back inside. Halfway through the door I find the damn thing, so I turn around to go back out. But I hear two people behind the counter talking about me. And one of them is calling me 'blowsy'!"

"Blowsy?"

"Yes! Can you believe the gall, Alice? I haven't heard that word used in years. *Blowsy.* Me! I'll be damned if I'm blowsy . . . I'm not, am I, Alice?"

"No, of course not, Nora. You are definitely not."

"Thank you. Now I can feed you."

"No," I said quickly, "not now." I handed her a copy of the photo I had taken from Amanda's apartment, which I had had duplicated only two hours ago on a color copier.

"Who are these people?" she asked, holding the photo at a distance to accommodate her worsening eyesight.

"Forget about the man. But the woman is Amanda Avery."

"Oh, my. Your old friend. That poor woman who was ice-picked trying to ransom her cat."

"Exactly."

"You knew her well, right?"

"Fairly well."

She tried to hand the picture back to me.

"No, Nora. I want you to keep it."

"Why? I didn't know her."

"Right. I know. But I need your help."

"Oh, no." All the breath seemed to go out of her. "Oh, Alice, you're getting involved in something. I can sense it."

"Look, Nora, all I want you to do is ask around about her."

"But I thought the lady taught Jane Austen or something up at Mount Holyoke. She was a professor. That isn't exactly the world I move in, Alice."

"Actually, she taught at Smith College. And her passion was for Virginia Woolf. She was never a professor, just a lowly adjunct when she was fired. And she'd been living in Manhattan for the past few years."

"So?"

"So I think she was involved in the theater."

"Oh. But, again . . . so?"

"So I think you should just show this photo around. You know what I mean, Nora. Ask the usual suspects."

"Musical theater?"

"Not sure."

"Acting classes? Playwrighting?"

"Don't know."

"Stripper?"

"Hardly, Nora."

She heaved a big sigh. Nora anchored the photo on her desk with a drinking glass. "Are you sure you're not lying to me, Alice?"

"About what?"

"About me being blowsy. I mean, I try to stay in shape, but—"

"Girl Scouts' honor, my friend."

She laughed. "I happen to know that while you definitely are a farm girl, Alice Nestleton, you were never a Girl Scout."

"True but trivial. *You are not blowsy!*"

"Thank you."

At three o'clock that afternoon I met Tony at a Starbuck's on Twenty-third Street. He had given up brandy temporarily and developed an addiction for mochachino with whipped cream.

Typical stage designer that he was, he could not sit at a table without constantly rearranging the objects in front of him: cup, napkin, sugar packets, spoon, whatever. He was fiddling with all those things when I sat down across from him. When he looked up, I could tell he was angry. His eyebrows seemed to meet in the middle of his forehead.

"What's eating you?" I asked.

"You damn well know."

"I damn well don't, Tony. I haven't the foggiest idea."

"It is obvious," he began in a stentorian voice, "you

have tired of me as a lover. Do you expect me to feel good about it?"

"Tony, what on earth are you talking about?"

"You don't have time to visit me. You don't invite me to stay over at your place anymore. Do you think I'm a fool? Do you imagine I don't know what's happening?"

"I am taking care of two apartments now, Basillio—mine and Amanda's—feeding two sets of animals, including an old dog who has to be walked several times a day. I am trying to find a home for Jake and Good Girl." The pitch of my voice was steadily mounting. "I simply don't have time for anything else right now. Believe me, I am not tired of you as a lover—I'm just tired, period."

He cocked his head, as if trying to evaluate my explanation. I figured it had passed muster when the hard line of his lips began to soften. "Okay, okay," he muttered. "No luck with the beasts, huh?"

"No one wants them."

"Then they've got to go to a shelter, Swede."

"It'll be a cold day in hell when that happens."

"I tried to find someplace for them, Swede, but nobody's interested."

"I appreciate that, Tony. But now I need your help on something else."

I placed the photo on the table.

"Amanda?" he asked.

"Yes."

"That her dead husband?"

"Yes."

"What's up?"

"I think Amanda wasn't quite what she appeared."

"Who is?"

"Tony, did the police question you?"

"Yeah. They think I made those calls from a pay phone on Carmine Street. They think you and I are in cahoots. I told them you double-crossed me and I never saw a penny of the seventy-five hundred you owe me from the ransom."

"Very funny."

"I thought you'd like it."

"Tony, I know the cat was kidnapped. I know just what happened—I was there. But it's all so unreal to me. Like something out of a children's book."

"Yeah. Fifteen thousand to get a cat back *is* unreal. Besides, I don't know any children's books that end with the main character getting stabbed in the back with an ice pick."

I pushed the photo closer to him.

"All right," he said, "so what am I supposed to do with this? What do you want?"

"Theatrical connection."

"Her?"

"Um. I'm not quite sure what she was doing, but she may have had directorial ambitions."

"So does Robert Redford."

"Show the picture around, Tony. See what you can turn up."

"And what else do I have to do?" he asked bitterly.

I took hold of his hand as he reached out to take the photograph. We sat there like that for a long time, holding hands, his mocha drink going cold, the fake whipped cream atomizing and vanishing into the liquid.

At nine that evening I met with Sam Tully in one of his unspeakably seedy bars. The poor man seemed to be obsessed with taverns that no sane person would consider going into. I believe he scours the city looking for new ones.

The one I met him in that evening was on Tenth Avenue in the low Twenties, a long way from his apartment on Spring Street, at the western fringe of Soho.

There he was, ensconced in a booth, smoking, drinking bourbon, talking to himself—or was he singing?—in other words, in his glory. The walls of the tavern were covered with old photos of the New York waterfront in its heyday, when cargo ships docked and rough working men unloaded them.

The moment I sat down, Sam asked me excitedly, "How do you like the place, doll? It's a great joint, isn't it?"

"Lovely, Sam." I didn't want to antagonize him because he hadn't wanted to meet me in the first place. He had been unusually fractious.

"Are you mad at me, Sam?" I asked.

Lydia Adamson

He looked into his drink, sheepish. His stubbled face and close-cropped gray head made him look like a sort of goofy geriatric Jean Genet. He was wearing a sleeveless quilted vest over a T-shirt—no coat. His intake of alcohol, he claimed, made him impervious to the cold, and the heat for that matter.

"No, no," he protested. "I just figured you were going to hassle me about taking that dog in."

"Well, you were wrong. I've already accepted the fact that you don't want that sweet old bitch."

"Don't? No, not *don't. Can't!* Pickles would eat her alive. Literally. No joke."

"That is absolutely ridiculous, Tully."

"Honey, believe me. Leopards eat dogs. Don't you ever read books? In Africa and Asia leopards go into villages at night. You know what they're after? Not noodle soup. Dogs, honey—dogs! Pickles may be one of those 'little people' leopards, but he'd make a meal out of that doggie fast."

Oh, that old man could be exasperating.

"If I told you once, Sam, I told you a dozen times, Pickles is not a midget leopard."

"Honey, if it looks like a duck and waddles like a duck . . ."

"Wait, Sam! Yes, he does have leopard-type spots. But he's a house cat. He's a new breed called Bengal cat. They're no relation to leopards. Not even their wild progenitors. Pickles's people came from India. A small wild cat more closely related to the ocelot or the lynx than the leop-

58

ard. You know all this. Why do you persist in a fantasy? Pickles would no more eat Good Girl than you would."

"I don't want to argue with you, Nestleton."

"Good."

I pulled out the photo and dropped it onto the table, in front of his nose.

He squinted. "This the dead lady?"

"That's her."

"Pretty. Looks like a woman I used to go with. Her name was Bella. She ran an employment agency down on Warren Street."

"I have a feeling, Sam."

"About what?"

"About Amanda. About what happened to her."

"Yeah?"

"It happened, of course. But maybe not the way I saw it."

"What you see is what you get."

"Maybe."

Then I told him about the *Mrs. Dalloway* affair.

"I mark up books, too, Nestleton, and no one says I want to be in the theater. When I was a kid, my copy of Sartre's *Nausea* looked like a lunatic's detailed road map with red stars for dangerous rail crossings."

He snatched the photo off the table and stared at it intently in the tavern's gloom.

"You want me to do something, honey. Spit it out."

"Okay. It isn't easy, Sam. But let me tell you what I'm thinking. I'm wondering if Amanda Avery stayed in the apartment all the time during her two years in New York. Was she reclusive? Did she go to the library? Movies? Museums? Maybe she stayed in during the day, working, and went out at night. Maybe with her husband. Maybe alone. Maybe only after he died. And maybe only in her own neighborhood—the only one in New York she knew. You know that area, Sam."

"Yeah, I do."

"It's chock-full of upscale restaurants and plenty of genteel bars a woman could walk into alone without feeling like Mae West."

"I'm getting your drift, Nestleton."

"Good."

"You want me to spruce up a bit?"

"Right."

"And barhop with all those beautiful people?"

"Exactly. Particularly First Avenue from about Fifty-seventh Street down to the U.N."

"So you're telling me, honey, that we're on a case."

"Sort of."

"No such animal, this 'sort of.' As Harry Bondo used to say . . . I think he said it in *Only the Dead Wear Socks* . . . 'If there's pork in your chopped sirloin, the only way to get rid of it is to eat it.' "

I suppressed a laugh. "But Tully, now that you're in the

process of creating a kinder, gentler Harry Bondo, maybe you ought to retire his sensibility, also."

"Funny you should use that word, Nestleton."

"What word?"

"Sensibility. Because Harry once said—now this is from the second book, I think—'I keep my sensibilities on my key ring.' "

I laughed out loud then. "Oh, that Harry."

"He's got a way with words, don't he?"

I walked out of the tavern and took a cab to Amanda's to check on the orphaned beasties. I had accomplished what I set out to do. Now we'll see, I thought. Let the chips fall where they may.

Aha. Another cliché.

Chapter 5

In fact, the chips fell so hard and so fast they took my breath away. They were falling at approximately twenty-four-hour intervals.

Before the first one fell, however, I found myself caught up in a form of mania because I believed that more extreme measures were needed to save Jake and Good Girl.

At the time, Woolworth's was closing all of its stores and conducting final sales.

I strode into a huge Woolworth's on Fourteenth Street and loaded up on drawing paper, oak tag, colored pencils, crayons, rolls of tape, and boxes of thumbtacks.

Then, as Bushy and Pancho watched me warily, I cleared off all the junk on my dining table and began to construct posters and notices leading toward the adoption of Mr. Jake and Ms. Good Girl.

I did modest ones and wild ones. I advertised them as a sophisticated cat/dog couple who must be adopted together. I did tearful notices for single adoptions. I did funny ones (I thought so, anyway) calling them a remarkable song and dance team. I characterized Jake in one as a cat with the most resplendent coat ever sprung from the feline gene pool. In another, I claimed that Good Girl could cook, count, and take herself for a walk.

I guess I went a bit bananas.

Then I began to put my creations up—on supermarket bulletin boards, in laundromats, on lampposts, scaffolds, and the sides of buildings.

I limited myself to two neighborhoods: my own and Amanda's. I ran into only one problem, and that occurred in my part of town.

That problem was an old woman who lived in my neighborhood and was known as The Enforcer.

It is illegal to post notices on lampposts, street signs, buildings, etc. But the law is ignored as long as the sign posted does not obscure the function of the post. Believe me, I put the posters up on the base of the objects, fighting for space with other citizens advertising guitar lessons, used baby carriages, phone sex, concert tickets—to name just a few offerings.

The Enforcer, however, in her misguided mission of

civic virtue, made her rounds daily and ripped down as many flyers as she could, given her somewhat feeble condition.

It was a longtime vendetta with her and she seemed to fix on my route, for some reason. I would turn around and see her three blocks back, tearing down what I had just posted.

Then I would circle back and repost my ads. Ah, it was a mad scene.

Being much younger than she, I finally wore her out. I imagine she went home to brood. Actually, I didn't hate her; she had her own peculiar vision of good citizenship.

When Nora called, I was in my loft, making more posters. I let the answering machine pick up. In fact, I hadn't answered my phone since I began my poster barrage.

There had been calls from potential cat-sitting clients, from friends, and even from my agent, who was wondering if I wanted to audition for a voice-over commercial for Czech motorcycles. They needed, she said, "a husky, dusky, sexy, mature voice."

I did pick up on Nora when I heard her saying: "Amanda—was that her name?"

"Yes!" I barked into the phone.

"No need to shout, Alice."

"Sorry."

"So you're there. Okay, because I have some very good news for you."

"I could use some good news, Nora. You don't know how badly I need some. Give it to me—dollop by dollop."

"Do you know Bobby Rinaldo?"

"No."

"He's an old dancer. In fact, he was one of the Sharks in the original *West Side Story*. Now he runs a dance studio on Eighth Avenue. He comes into the bistro with friends pretty regularly. He was in the other night. I sat down at his table for a few minutes, like I always do. Then I remembered that photo you gave me. So I showed it to him."

"Don't tell me: he knew Amanda."

"Yes. Said she was a well-known student at the studio. She took the whole range of classes—jazz, tap, Afro-Cuban, you name it. But—and this is a pretty big 'but'—" She paused there.

"But what?" I pressed.

"Well, when I told him her name, he began to waffle. Said maybe he was mistaken. Because the woman he knew was about this one's age and was a dead ringer for her, but her name wasn't Amanda. It was Lucrezia. Lucrezia Smith. Isn't that a weird name?"

"When did she attend?"

"Bobby says she's been at the studio on and off for the past two years or so."

"Nora, are you sure that's the name he gave you—Lucrezia Smith?"

"Yes, I'm sure. It's such a crazy name, how could I forget it?"

"I suppose you're right. Well, thank you for the good work."

"Does it help you?"

"I think it might. I'll be in touch."

I hung up then. I didn't know what the information meant, except that it proved my speculation that there was some kind of intense theatrical relationship between Amanda and the novel *Mrs. Dalloway*.

After all, Lucrezia Smith is the name of a major character in the book. She is the Italian wife of a young Englishman who is going mad.

I went back to my poster making. There had been no responses to my pleas, so I planned to expand into another neighborhood, namely Chelsea.

The second chip fell while I was at my artwork. A call from Tony.

I picked up the moment I heard his voice. I didn't want to exacerbate his feelings of rejection. (Sometimes I'm such an old-fashioned girl, I surprise myself.)

"First, let's get something straight," Tony said forthrightly. "I'm not calling for sex, food, or companionship."

"Okay."

"What are you doing?"

"I'm still trying to get Jake and Good Girl adopted. I'm putting up signs all over the city, one neighborhood at a time."

"Need help?"

"Not right now."

"Oh. Well, listen, you want to hear a funny story?"

"Sure." (Not really true, but, as I said, I felt I owed him some attention.)

"Remember about a year ago I went to a posh loft party down in Soho? On Wooster Street. And I met a beautiful young actress?"

"No, Basillio, I don't."

"Yeah, you do. I told you all about it. But let me refresh your memory."

"Do that. I don't remember."

"We're not getting any younger, are we, Swede? Anyway, this young woman at the party seemed to develop a hunger for me. And I mean a hunger. On the way out of the party I had to physically defend myself against her advances."

I laughed. "I recall it now, Tony. You were in one of your brief fidelity phases."

"Brief? What do you mean? I'm always faithful to you, Swede. Alice's Launcelot."

"In your fashion."

"Of course. Let me get back to the story. The party happened a year ago. Now cut to the present. Yesterday, to be precise. Late in the afternoon. I'm strolling downtown in the brisk autumnal weather. Going to have coffee with a guy I know who works at a casting office. I get to Ninth

Lydia Adamson

Street, little east of Second Avenue, and I'm looking into one of those boutique windows.

"Lo and behold, I see her—*her*. Standing in the doorway of this dress shop, smoking a cigarette. Obviously she works there. So I say to her, 'Well, at least it's better than waitressing.' She remembers me, to say the least; she smiles at me like I have a million bucks in my pocket. Now, to be honest, I'm a bit lonely. Not to lay a guilt trip on you or anything, but, you know, men will be men.

"We chat. She still digs me. I don't know what to do. So I get to telling her the story of what I'm doing to help you out, and I whip out the photo and show it to her—all just to keep the conversation out of the path of the erotic. And you know what she says? She says, 'Oh my God. What are you doing with her photograph?'

"It turns out that they had both taken a class at Marymount College. A class in songwriting. Do you believe it? Pop songwriting. Taught by—well, I forget who—some music big shot. But she says to me that Sally Seton was a very nice older woman, a good student who was really serious about the class. Wait a minute, I tell her, that can't be right. This lady in the photograph is named Amanda, not Sally. But she says no, no, it's Sally Seton. She ought to know the woman she sat next to all those weeks in the class. What could I do? The woman in the picture can't be two different people, right? But I almost hit a home run for you, Swede. Didn't I?"

"They are the same person, Tony."

68

"Sally Seton is Amanda Avery?"

"Exactly."

"Then your friend was mighty strange."

"Go on with your story, Tony."

"That's all there is."

"And the young actress who wants you so badly?"

"I left her there, of course. In the shop."

"You left with her number in your pocket, if I know you."

"You malign me, madam. Call me when you want me."

Well, that was that. Bizarre as it sounded, Amanda's double life—make that triple life—sounded totally believable. More believable, anyway, than the things I'd seen and heard with my own eyes and ears on the night Amanda was murdered.

Now I had to apply myself to the "why" of her multiple identities. Why would she take dance classes and sign up as Lucrezia Smith? Why pass herself off in the songwriting class as Sally Seton—another important character from *Mrs. Dalloway*?

Sally Seton was in fact Clarissa Dalloway's childhood companion.

But I couldn't devote any more attention to the Amanda puzzle right then. I had to get back to the posters.

Chip number three came in the form of a portly, disheveled old mystery writer—none other than Sam Tully. Here's what happened:

I was at the Beekman Place apartment. It was about ten in the evening and I was tired and grumpy. I picked up around the place and laid out fresh food and water for the animals.

The copy of *Mrs. Dalloway* was clearly visible, on the sofa. I was just staring at it malevolently.

I had to tell the beasts the brutal truth: that there were no takers so far; that no one in this vast, ordinarily compassionate, multicultural city seemed to want anything to do with them.

I confessed to Good Girl that I had lied shamelessly about her powers and abilities, implying that she could do everything but bake corn muffins, but even that had not helped.

I confessed to Jake that I had characterized him as a feline of unique and awesome beauty, but to no avail.

I closed my little speech to the two bored audience members with the promise that I would continue my efforts, no matter what.

The telephone rang then.

"It's me—Sam. On the case, doll. Couldn't get you at home, figured you were at the dead lady's pad. There's trouble, Nestleton."

"What trouble?"

"I've been working all evening, honey. Six, seven, eight bars on First Avenue. Flashing that damned photo. I come up with nothing. And I'm getting looped."

"You weren't supposed to actually drink in every one of the bars you canvassed, Sam."

"Keep quiet and listen, doll."

"All right."

"I'm on Fifty-first and First right now."

"Okay."

"I'm at a pay phone."

"Okay."

"And I think I found the Avery dame's watering hole. I'm looking right at it. I got the juice now, I got the feeling. The dead lady was in this place."

"So go on in, Tully. Check it out."

There was a silence.

"Sam . . . are you still there?"

"Yeah. I'm here. I can't go in there, honey. Not alone."

"What are you talking about, Tully? You spend time at bars that Wyatt Earp wouldn't go in."

"It's hard to explain," he said nervously. "This place is— well, it's like eating snails. I just can't do it."

"You want me with you?"

"Yeah. Come on over here, doll."

"I'll be there in ten minutes."

I made it in nine. Sam was shivering by the pay phone. I couldn't believe what he looked like.

I'd told him to "spruce up." What he had done was just slip a tie around his neck, over his vest and T-shirt. It was a ridiculously wide orange tie with a knot that was more like

71

a noose. Completing his spruce look was a hat that looked like an abandoned prop from a George Raft movie.

"What is it, honey? What are you looking at me like that for? You look like you just saw a ghost."

I didn't answer. Sam pointed to the bar in question then. It was a place called Bell, Book & Cabernet.

I could instantly see why he was loathe to enter the place alone. It was too ridiculous for words—a bar/restaurant that tried to achieve a distinctive elegance by aping an Edwardian gentlemen's club. Claret-hued carpeting. A forest of weathered dark wood. Rich leather armchairs. Hunting scenes on the walls.

"Do you know what I mean now?" Sam asked. "Some places make even a brave man shudder. They're just too . . . too . . . against the grain, against history, against booze. You know what I mean? They're just—"

"It's all right, Tully. Calm yourself. I get the picture. Let's go in together. You may find the place horrific and an insult to drunks everywhere, but I agree with you that to a lady from Beloit via Northampton, it might have spelled peace and tranquility."

We went inside. There were intimate little alcoves along the wall across from the bar, which stretched for miles and was made of magnificent cherrywood. Behind the bar was a huge mirror with tinted glass. The stock was displayed like flowers. Past the bar were the swinging doors that led to the restaurant area.

Three people sat drinking up front, and a couple in one of the alcoves were holding hands across the table. All was hushed. From somewhere in the back, or somewhere in the ether, very very softly, came the voice of Sarah Vaughan—a bit incongruous.

A young woman in what bordered on formal evening wear approached us carrying menus. Her scrunched-up little mouth said she was not pleased.

"We'd just like some drinks," I said preemptively.

"I'm afraid the gentleman cannot be seated. We require jackets." There was sadness in her voice, but I didn't buy it for a minute.

I pulled her aside. "He has a severe skin disorder," I explained, my voice an embarrassed whisper. "He cannot tolerate any fabric on his arms."

The woman looked at me—hard—and then at Sam. Finally she sighed resignedly and led us to the end of the bar.

The bartender approached. He was dressed like a valet in an old black-and-white film—not young. There was not a flicker of disapproval, or anything else for that matter, in his expression. He was gracious as could be as he asked us what we'd like.

I ordered cranberry juice with a slice of lime. Sam asked for Wild Turkey "straight up" and some unpronounceable Czech beer that was the house brand on tap.

The drinks were served in exquisite, thick-sided Swedish crystal. Underneath each drink the bartender slipped a monogrammed napkin. We toasted to something or other,

Sam and I, clinking our glasses lightly. I was going to share with Sam a snide comment about our surroundings, but suddenly the bartender was back in front of us, staring intently, almost insanely, at Sam.

"Is it possible," he stammered, "that I have the honor of serving Mr. Samuel Tully?"

Sam and I exchanged incredulous glances. Then he faced the bartender again. "I am Tully," he said.

"The creator of Harry Bondo? Author of *Only the Dead Wear Socks*?"

"Yeah."

The staid bartender uttered a little whoop of delight.

I turned to my companion. "Tully, I would never have guessed—I mean, I never realized you were famous."

"Either did I, Nestleton."

"I saw you on video, a cable TV show," the bartender said. "It was done at Rutgers University a few years ago. A group of mystery writers were reading from their work. You brought the house down."

"First and last time I ever did that," Sam replied sheepishly.

"So what has become of the Bondo books? I kept looking for them, but there were no more."

"Terminated—with extreme prejudice," said Sam. "But there may be a resurrection."

"Wait! Wait there!" the bartender implored, as if we were about to leave, which we weren't.

He rushed over to a cabinet, hunted around inside it, and came back with two tattered paperback books—Harry Bondo mysteries. He opened each to the title page and then pushed them across the bar along with a ball-point pen.

"You want me to sign it 'Harry' or 'Sam'?"

"Sam."

"What's your name?"

"James Durbin."

Sam autographed the books and pushed them back into the bartender's waiting hands. Mr. Durbin broke into a huge grin. "You know, I've been working on a mystery story myself."

"Is that so?" Tully said.

"Yes. I've got a lady police officer—small, smart, pretty, Latin. Very tough. She's hunting a killer—a bartender. His MO is demonic. He never stays at a job for very long. Before he quits, he always murders one male customer who drinks vodka martinis. The lady cop first has to decipher the pattern of the killings; then the pattern of the killer's employment; then the configuration of the relationships between victims and killer. Meanwhile, her marriage falls apart, she falls in love with a psycho, she's investigated by Internal Affairs, and she's becoming addicted to Demerol after a painful operation to correct her hammertoes."

We were silent. Sam looked to be in shock. I felt a nudge on my leg. I looked down to see him slipping me Amanda's photograph. Obviously he thought I was the one who should make the inquiry. He had a point.

"What's the lady cop's name?" Tully asked.

"Sonya."

"Good name. I like it."

"And the killer, the bartender, has fifty aliases. But his favorite one is Winston."

"How does he kill?"

"Strychnine in the martini glass."

"Why does he do it?"

Durbin was taken aback. "You know better than I, Mr. Tully. Remember what Harry Bondo told that gold shield in book one: 'Look for motive, buster, and the only thing you'll find is a pickpocket.' "

"Did Bondo really say that?" Sam asked. He looked mortally perplexed, or perhaps he had had one Wild Turkey too many.

"Of course he said it," Durbin replied. He then picked up the autographed books and brought them back to the cabinet for safe storage.

It was time. I slipped off the stool and walked down the bar to where Durbin was secreting his treasures.

"Mr. Durbin, I need your help," I said.

He straightened.

"We came here to find an old friend. Her number is unlisted. We were supposed to meet up with her. She didn't show. All we know is that she might have come in here once in a while."

It was a mélange of truth and lies.

"What's her name?" he asked.

"Amanda." I slid the photo across the bar to him, wondering if I should also have mentioned her pseudonyms: Lucrezia and Sally.

It didn't matter, though. He responded the moment he looked down at the picture. "Oh, yes. I know her. She used to come in regularly, perhaps twice a week. White Bordeaux. Never more than one glass."

"When was the last time you saw her here?"

"About two months ago. I remember, she came in alone."

"Didn't she always come in alone?"

"No. Not at all. She was usually with a young man." He pointed to Ivan Tasso's face. "Not him, whoever that is. The man I mean was a lot younger. A playwright, I believe."

"And his name?"

"Lyman? No, Lyle. Last name, I don't know. I should remember it, too, because last year he gave me a ticket to his play. It's a bit embarrassing not to recall . . . Wait."

He rushed back to the cabinet, and after a minute of rummaging pulled out a *Playbill*, which he placed in front of me.

Synchronicity: A Bedroom Farce
by Lyle Engel

I had a vague recollection of the title and tried to visualize the ad that had run in the papers last year. *"Funny. Erotic. A talented young four-person cast."* Or something like that. Yes, it had garnered rather good reviews, but had only a brief run in one of the Theatre Row houses, all the way west on Forty-second Street.

I flipped through the Playbill. The producer, it said, was Red Lion Productions in association with—and I did a double-take—Joan Engel.

It was startling to have a name I knew in connection with Amanda jump out at me like that.

Was this young playwright, Lyle, Joan Engel's son or something? Perhaps a nephew? And, even more interesting, had Joan Engel and Harvey Stith known about the relationship between Amanda and young Lyle?

Amanda and *young* Lyle. Was it possible? Was the prim Amanda Avery cheating on her husband with an attractive young man? Or did I just have a dirty mind?

I found that I was staring stupidly at the *Playbill*. What did all this have to do with a kidnapped cat? Or with *Mrs. Dalloway*? Connections, Alice, connections! I had light-bulbs but no lamps.

"Thank you for this," I said, handing the booklet back to James Durbin. I went back and took my seat next to Sam.

"This is the second time tonight I've seen that crazy expression on your face, doll," he remarked. "Did you see another ghost?"

"No ghost, Sam. More like a skeleton."

"She was here, right?"

"Oh yes. Often. And not alone."

He nodded. "What do we got?"

"Maybe a new script."

"Nestleton," he said, smirking, "the lady's dead. Scripts don't mean a damn thing."

His comment infuriated me. I knocked over his drink. Then I began to sob. I was seeing Amanda holding the rescued harlequin Jake in her arms, seeing her crumple, that horrendous ice pick buried in her back.

I ran out of the place.

Tully caught up with me three blocks away.

"Don't you understand!" I yelled at him. "It was all a fake. She didn't die for a cat."

"Steady, Nestleton, steady. Just tell me what you want me to do."

"Go home, Sam. Get sober. Sleep. I'll need you in the morning."

Chapter 6

Some intersections in New York City bring out the young girl in me; the long-gone Alice just bursts into view.

One such intersection is the corner of Fifty-seventh Street and Seventh Avenue, at Carnegie Hall. Don't ask me why I get like that, there. I don't really know. Of course it has something to do with music and theater and dance and the ingenue in the big city for the first time. But it's more than that. I was a farm girl when I arrived in New York, the rough edges only slightly planed down by a stay in Minneapolis.

And what I saw . . . what I really saw the first time I stood on that corner was the notion of freedom. Freedom to do exactly what I wanted to do within the limits of my purse, my heart, my will, my talent, and my moral code.

Why that particular corner? Maybe because it was a kind of crossroads: to the south of it there were all the lights and promises of the theater district; to the north, the splendor of Central Park; west was the excitement of Hell's Kitchen; and to the east the opulence of Sutton Place.

Of course, the freedom I speak of turned out to be more or less illusory. But the morning after that revelatory visit to Bell, Book & Cabernet, as I stood on that corner with a disgruntled Sam Tully in tow, I had that same peculiar feeling—that I was on the cusp of some kind of discovery—on the edge of freedom.

All that should help to explain my slight giddiness as I walked into the Fisk Building, a towering structure at 57 West Fifty-seventh Street, just a few paces from Crossroads Corner.

"How do you know Joan Engel's here?" Sam asked. "You told me she lives near Beekman Place. Maybe she works out of her apartment. I mean, how do you know Red Lion Productions is her company? Do you got any idea what you're doing, honey? Maybe that cranberry juice you had last night messed you up. You probably couldn't handle the lime."

Poor hung-over Sam Tully. He didn't know the secret language of theater. After all, he was just a lovable old mystery writer. In the theater world, when you see a credit that says "Produced by John O. Smith and Purple People Eater Productions," they are always one and the same thing. Producers love to add on corporate entities, like hats. To be

81

sure, the corporate entity usually exists, in a legal sense. But it is a one-person operation.

I eased Sam's skepticism with a wink. He seemed to trust winks.

The office was on the ninth floor. As we left the elevator and approached the thick plate-glass doors, Sam asked, "By the way, what's my role here? Muscle?"

I chuckled and patted him on the arm. "I haven't figured that out yet."

Then we walked in. My stomach was doing some serious fluttering.

It was an oddly grim, sparse space. Nothing on the walls. Three standing files. A sofa. Two desks. And one Joan Engel.

She looked up from behind a desk, confused for a moment. Then she recognized me and smiled warmly.

"Good to see you, Alice. I've been asking Harvey how you're doing with Amanda's creatures. It's so sad, no one wants to adopt those animals. I did my best, honestly. I think you're wonderful to help out like this. It's a fabulous act of compassion. Maybe something good will happen. Who knows?"

I introduced her to Sam. For some unexplained reason, he gave a little bow, not unlike an Austrian duke.

"I didn't mean to barge in like this," I lied, "but something important has come up and I just had to ask you three questions."

She looked puzzled. As if it were quite impossible that our new relationship was deep enough to bring forth even one question. Still, she invited me to ask as many questions as I liked.

"First of all, Joan, is Lyle Engel, the playwright, related to you? And second, did you know he and Amanda were lovers? Third, did Harvey know?"

What happened next was most strange. She bent her head low, literally touching the surface of the desk, as if offering some sort of prayer. Then she looked up at Sam and me as if we were mob extortionists, the fear and desperation written clearly on her face.

Joan rose from her seat behind the desk then, walked to the office door, opened it, and in a hoarse, croaking voice, told us to "get out, stay out." I tried to speak and so did Tully. But she wasn't having it. Over and over, she said the same thing: "Get out, stay out . . . get out, stay out."

Five minutes later we were back at my crossroads corner. I don't know about Sam, but I was in a kind of daze.

He chuckled softly. "Guess she wasn't too crazy about those three questions," he said.

"I guess not. Maybe Harvey Stith will like them a little better."

I found a working pay phone but no quarters. Sam didn't have any coins either. We popped into four stores before a kindly merchant changed a dollar for us. Then I made the call.

Stith picked up fast, as he always did.

"It's Alice Nestleton," I said, but didn't get the chance to expand on that statement, because he slammed the phone down immediately.

"What happened?" Sam asked.

"He hung up on me."

"You're not too popular today, angel."

"Joan must have called him while we were looking for change."

"Called him? Why?"

"To tell him I was asking questions."

"Yeah. So?"

I didn't reply for a minute. When I did, "Sister Susie sat on the seashore sewing socks for soldiers and sailors," is what came out. "Remember that one, Tully?"

"Sure. But I always liked 'Peter Piper' better. What's the matter with you, Nestleton?"

"Say either of them fast and you stumble over the words. Isn't that right, Tully?"

His look asked the obvious question: *Are you nuts?*

"But we're not going to stumble anymore, are we, Tully?"

"We're not?"

"No. Because we know now what went down."

"We do?"

"Are you as fond of that phrase as I am, Tully? It's really popular these days. They don't say that a crime 'occurred' or 'happened.' They say it 'went down.' Do you like it?"

"Yeah, it's fine by me."

I prodded him to turn east on Fifty-seventh Street.

"Where we going?"

"To Amanda's."

"What for?"

"To think."

"Anything you say, honey. I'm with you."

To my surprise, Good Girl greeted Sam Tully like a long-lost friend, even though she'd never so much as seen him before.

"Where's the crazy cat?" he asked.

"Hiding somewhere, no doubt, way up high. Jake is not what you'd call a social butterfly. Have a seat, Sam."

In fact, we both sat down.

"Some nice place," he noted, looking around admiringly.

"Yes, it is. Her husband had money. Lots and lots of it."

The Gordon setter was climbing slowly up onto Sam's lap. He groaned.

"Are you comfortable, Sam?"

"Yeah."

"Good. I have a story to tell."

"I like stories as much as the next guy. But keep it short."

"I'll try," I said, and launched into the telling. "This woman, this erstwhile friend of mine—Amanda Avery—well, I thought I knew her. She was a reclusive, kind of straitlaced academic. She cared, I believed, about one thing: a critical work on Virginia Woolf which she never seemed able to finish, and if she had finished it, it would probably never be published. She and I are friends, but friends at a distance. We lose touch with each other—that happens. Then one day, out of the blue, I get a call from her. And guess what?"

"What?"

"It turns out she's been living in Manhattan for the past two years and she's married to the kind of man I would never in a million years have thought she would be with."

"Well, like you said, that kind of thing happens. People change their minds. My first wife said when we first met that she wouldn't be seen dead with me."

"Yes, a lot of things seemed to have just 'happened' in Amanda's case. Not only was she married, and widowed, and living only a short bus ride from me, but she was also taking a variety of classes—dance lessons, songwriting classes, what have you—under assumed names. And instead of devoting herself to her beloved Virginia Woolf manuscripts, she had stored them away. Then, in what is probably the most bizarre turn of all, she was having an affair with a kid playwright whom she met through two show business neighbors. Maybe the affair even dates back to before her wealthy husband died. It's all pretty strange, don't you think, Sam? Considering the kind of person I knew her to be."

"To say the least. Anyway . . . along comes Jake."

"Right. Along comes Jake. She takes him in because she's honoring her late husband's wishes. Or so she says."

"It's a nice story, honey. But where is it going?"

"Oh, I haven't told you the story yet, Sam. That was just the background. The story is yet to come."

"Oh. Okay." He nudged Good Girl gently off his lap and she reluctantly left his side.

I picked up the paperback *Mrs. Dalloway* and the sheaf of theater reviews and tossed them onto his lap. "Take a look at these," I said.

As he studied the papers I gave him a few pointers. "Check the underlining carefully, Sam. Look at the little comments. Those are the kind of things a director does when he's going over a script. And then look closely at the reviews. Notice that the preponderance of them deal with productions that have some kind of book—in other words, a storyline—as well as music."

Tully studied the items in silence. At last he put them aside. "Okay. Got it. So what?"

"Here's the script, Sam. Amanda Avery created a play with song and music and dance out of Virginia Woolf's novel *Mrs. Dalloway*. Even academics have one wild creative burst once in a while. And she prepared for it by dance classes and songwriting classes.

"Not only did this burst of creativity and passion make her feel good—a kind of liberation, one could say—but she realized it had enormous financial potential. Yes, I know:

Why should she need money? Her husband was wealthy. But maybe she wanted her own money; maybe it meant independence. Or maybe she just got the theater bug, bad. Anyway, she shows the work to some theater people she knows. They are excited also.

"At the last moment, however, Amanda withdraws the work, out of a kind of intellectual shame. She is murdered and the product of her labors is stolen. The cat kidnapping and ransom is set up as a way to mask the true motive for the murder."

There was a dead silence.

"Well? What do you think, Sam?" I prodded.

"Plausible, honey," he said, nodding.

Not the response I was hoping for. "Plausible? Is that all you can say!" I asked huffily. I thought I'd constructed a rather brilliantly logical scenario to explain the murder.

Sam shrugged. "I guess I can also say that you have a hell of an imagination. I mean, you've got a real talent for plotting."

"I object to your use of the word imagination, Tully. Everything I said fits perfectly. The thing fits! The problem is, what do I do now?"

"I take it that these show biz friends of the dead lady are Engel and Stith—and they're the ice pick crew."

"Exactly. Which is why she threw us out of her office that way, and why he hung up on me. They know I know."

"You may know . . . you may think you know . . . but you

don't have any gristle on the bone. None. This story of yours is all in your head. You got a lousy old marked-up paperback; a possible—okay, probable—affair between Avery and Engel's son or nephew or whatever . . . and . . . and . . ." He was searching for a word, I supposed. The one he settled on and used was a surprise: "Gossamer!" he exhaled. "Like the song says, 'gossamer wings.' "

"And gossamer wings don't interest the NYPD?"

"Not in this life, Nestleton."

"We have to think, Sam."

"Yeah."

"Let me feed Jake and Good Girl and then we'll share a cab downtown. I know you think better when you're moving."

"Yeah."

I refilled the dog's food and water bowls. Jake's were still full.

"He isn't eating," I said to Sam.

"Who?"

"Jake. The cat."

"When am I going to see that character?"

"In a minute," I promised.

It was a promise I couldn't keep. Jake was gone.

Chapter 7

We ransacked that apartment. I was tearing around like a crazy person. I could not believe Jake had vanished again.

Sam kept muttering: "The phone call is coming, honey. Get set for it. This time they'll want twenty thousand dollars. You got twenty thousand dollars?"

And I kept muttering back: "Shut up, Sam!"

By afternoon, Sam had abandoned the search. The exertion, along with last night's Wild Turkeys, had done him in.

But I kept going. I searched every closet, every drawer, every window, every shelf, the linings of every winter coat. I patted and I probed, I dug, I whistled and called and even sang. I squeaked like a mouse, I cooed like a mourning dove. But no Jake. He was gone. Gone!

Late in the afternoon, I finally collapsed on a chair in

the living room, across from the sofa where Sam was sleeping with his mouth open, guarded by a seemingly happy Good Girl.

The story's all in your head, Sam had said. The only thing in my head now was confusion. Was it really possible that Jake had been kidnapped *again*? By whom?

If I was correct in thinking the first kidnapping had been orchestrated by Stith and Engel as a diversion, then why would they do it again? Did they want to kill me now? Plausible, as Sam had said. I guessed that it was plausible they wanted me dead. But did they think the cat trick would work a second time?

Surely they knew I didn't have any money. The ransom demand would have to be fifteen dollars instead of fifteen thousand. Were Joan and Harvey crazy as well as evil?

And if it wasn't a catnapping—then how did Jake get out? How? The tops of the windows were kept open about an inch for circulation, but no full-grown cat could have squeezed through, and there was no other way out save the front door.

I gathered my strength, got off the chair, picked up the phone, and called Harvey Stith again.

I didn't allow him to hang up on me. Right off the bat, I began screaming at him: "You took the cat again, didn't you! You have a key to this apartment! What is there to gain this time around, Harvey? Don't you understand—I *know* what happened. I know what you two did!"

There was a pause, then a sigh, then he began to speak very softly. "I think you should seek help immediately, Alice. Joan told me you seemed to be in an emotional crisis when you visited her. That's why I hung up this morning—I thought it best not to upset you further. Joan and I have both been in the theater long enough to know that a hysterical out-of-work actress is best left alone; friends cannot help at such a time. It's a job for a qualified therapist.

"As for taking the cat . . . I've been in Boston the last few days. I arrived home just in time to get Joan's call saying that you broke into her office this morning with a thug. Take my advice, Alice. Seek help. It's never too late."

He gently replaced the receiver then.

I let Tully sleep. Good Girl seemed to be enjoying the sound of his snoring.

I sat down amid the rubble and tried to focus my thoughts—not much luck with that.

When Tully came to, it was dark and the wind was blowing something fierce off the East River.

"Find him, Nestleton?" he asked, yawning.

"No, Tully, I didn't. He's gone."

"What do you want to do now?"

"Eat. Let's go get some dinner and then start searching for him."

"Where?"

"The neighborhood."

"What about the hallway? He might be right out in the hallway."

"There *is* no hallway, Tully. Remember? The door opens onto the street. And I don't know how to get into the cellar."

"They got a garden out back?"

"Garden! Sam, behind the far wall of the house it's a sheer drop onto the East River Drive."

"Oh. What about the roof?"

"That's a thought. But I have no idea how to get up there."

"That's a problem, honey."

"Of course, if he really has been kidnapped again, what's the point of looking?"

"Right."

"But we've got to look. Somehow I have the feeling he wasn't taken this time. I jumped the gun, accusing Joan and Harvey."

"Right," he said wearily.

So we took to the street and poked around. Admittedly, the search was halfhearted. We were taking the lids off of recycling bins and peering in, checking dark doorways and calling into alleys. We queried a few doormen, who were polite but rather patronizing. Finally we climbed down to one of the small "vest-pocket" parks that overhang the Drive and interrogated the homeless souls who camp out there because Beekman Place is a nice safe neighborhood.

"This is for the birds, doll," Tully said in defeat. "It's too dark to spot him anyway."

"But the eyes, Sam. You can see his eyes in the dark."

"Yeah. Sure. Why can't you look at it this way, Nestleton: now you don't have to worry about finding someone to adopt him."

His comment ended the search. We went to a neighborhood luncheonette for a bite of dinner.

"I'm going to have to call the agencies in the morning," I announced.

"What agencies?"

"All the animal shelters that have hotlines for missing pets. If you find a stray—a stray anything—you call these places. They record it. If you lose a pet, you call them. They record it."

"But will you love me in the morning?" Sam asked.

"*What?* What kind of nonsense are you talking, Sam? What does it have to do with missing pets?"

I was immediately sorry for that outburst, and softened my tone accordingly. Poor Tully was cracking under the pressure—and was possibly still hung over.

"What was that you just asked me, doll?"

"Never mind, Sam. It doesn't matter. Let's get into a cab and go downtown. I've had it."

It had been such a long and ugly day that when I got home I didn't say a word to Bushy and Pancho. I fed them, showered within an inch of my life, and, wearing a scuzzyfuzzy old 1950s-type sorority girl nightgown, fell into the arms of Morpheus, where I dreamed the kind of dreams no sorority girl should ever know.

The next morning, I was a lot more civil to my beloved cattys. I treated myself as well: I made Swedish pancakes with real butter and maple syrup. The devil made me do it. I was finishing the last delectable morsel when I realized I had forgotten to put up "Lost Cat" posters in the Beekman Place area. But the neighborhood was already littered with my adoption posters—I was becoming a public menace.

At 8:00 A.M. sharp I began calling the animal agency hotlines in Manhattan. I knew the drill. I had been through it all before. Call the ASPCA, the Humane Society, Bide-A-Wee, Abide, and the three or four others who maintain hotlines for lost pets. Give your name, address, phone number. Tell who is lost. Where and when the animal was last seen. All data are dutifully noted, all computer records checked.

No critter answering Jake's description had shown up anywhere—so far.

I made myself a cup of Medaglia d'Oro instant espresso. No matter how much sugar I added, it was bitter.

Soon the tears began to roll down my face. No, not because of the coffee. Not for myself at all. For Jake.

Where was that fool of a cat? Where was the mysterious, cool, funny-colored feline? Was he in harm's way?

Oh! He had to be. Whether he'd been kidnapped or simply fled.

I didn't know what else to do, but I had to do something . . . anything. So I began phoning animal shelters in the other four boroughs: Brooklyn, Queens, the Bronx, and Staten Island. Most had no official hotline like the ones in Manhattan. But I kept going, working off the Yellow Pages.

On the twelfth call—or perhaps it was the eleventh—a most remarkable conversation occurred.

The person at the other end of the line was a Mr. Garcia. The shelter was in Jackson Heights, Queens. The name of the facility was Little Flower.

GARCIA: The best I can do is post it on our bulletin board.

NESTLETON: That would be fine. The cat was lost in Beekman Place, on the Manhattan side of the bridge, just south of—

GARCIA (interrupting): I know where Beekman Place is, Miss. (Laughs) You think it swam the river and then got on the E train?

NESTLETON: Anyway, his name is Jake. Smallish, shorthaired, with a strange coat. One side is tan, the other is charcoal. And the color scheme is totally symmetrical. Same thing with the face.

Here the conversation ended, temporarily. Because there was no response at all from Mr. Garcia. He had fallen completely silent. I figured he was busy writing down what I was saying, so I gave him time. But after a minute or two, still no sound.

NESTLETON: Are you there, Mr. Garcia?

GARCIA: Of course I'm here. Where do you think I am? But I'll tell you something, Miss. I believe you're pulling my leg.

NESTLETON: That's ridiculous. I wouldn't play a prank like that on anyone.

GARCIA: Okay. But you just gave me a description of Willie Sutton.

NESTLETON: What are you talking about? Who's Willie Sutton?

GARCIA: You're too young to remember, probably. He was a bank robber. A lousy bank robber. He was always getting caught. But he was a great escape artist. Whatever jail they locked him up in, he got out of it. Anyway, the cat you describe is known to a whole lot of people. We call him Willie Sutton because he's always getting caught, getting adopted, and then getting away.

NESTLETON: How can you be so sure Jake is Willie Sutton?

GARCIA: I never heard of another cat with that kind of coat.

NESTLETON: But how does he keep getting out?

GARCIA: Sometimes the window. Sometimes a vent. But he's famous for his shadow trick.

NESTLETON: What's that?

GARCIA: Imagine you're about to leave your apartment. You open the door. Just before you shut the light, you check things. All seems fine—faucets closed, oven's off, and so on. There's the cat, fast asleep on the rug. Or so it seems. You flip the light switch and head out. At that moment your "sleeping" cat zooms off the rug. You hear nothing, see nothing. He ends up just behind you, in your shadow, so to speak. You have no idea he's there. He stays in that shadow zone until you start locking the door. Then he flies off while you're distracted—down the hall, into the basement, whatever. Get it? The shadow trick. It seems Willie Sutton is a master at it.

NESTLETON: I don't know what to say.

GARCIA: Look at it this way. It's an honor. I mean, the cat is a legend in his own time.

I thanked Mr. Garcia profusely, hung up the receiver, and just sat there in a kind of shock.

I tried to think. I couldn't fit the data anywhere. If Jake was indeed "Willie Sutton," the feline escape artist, what did it have to do with my theory that Harvey Stith and Joan Engel lured Amanda into a trap and then murdered her, using the cat as the bait? Did it trash the theory? Enhance it? If so, how?

And why didn't the people at Abide tell Amanda that Jake was Willie Sutton? Or didn't they know?

Of course, they had discouraged her a bit. I had to

admit that much; I was standing right there. But they certainly could have been more adamant. It was perfectly reasonable to expect them to tell us about Willie Sutton, if they knew his story.

I had a sudden impulse to call the director of Abide and give him or her a piece of my mind.

Then I calmed down. After all, Abide was an animal shelter, not a prison farm or a psychiatric unit. Abide didn't have the resources to compile personality profiles on the animals they rescued and placed.

Bush was beginning to carry on. He wanted to be brushed. Pancho ceased his running to and fro long enough to stare contemptuously at his colleague. Panch never complained about anything, really. No excuses. No remorse. No regrets.

I reached for the grooming brush. The telephone rang.

It was Gloria Avery—the last person I wanted to speak to just then.

"Are you well, Alice?" she asked.

"I'm well. But the cat—Jake, that is—has vanished from the apartment and I haven't yet been able to find a home for the dog."

"I don't care about the dog or the bloody cat," she snapped. "I have something I must show you."

"Of course. Can you mail it?"

"Why mail? I'm not calling from Beloit. I'm in New York."

Lydia Adamson

"Oh?"

"I can be at your place in twenty minutes."

"Okay." I gave her the address and instructions on how to get here, and then added, sounding a bit absurd, I suppose: "Are you going to want coffee?"

"I don't need coffee," she replied brusquely, "I need your help. Just plain old-fashioned help. Don't you people know what that means?" *Click!*

My, they grew some imperious women out there in Wisconsin! I picked up Bushy's brush. And just what the hell did she mean by "you people"?

I began to brush my beautiful, vain, slightly overweight Maine coon.

"You're no Willie Sutton," I told him. "That's for sure."

Chapter 8

Gloria must have taken a cab. She arrived in less than fifteen minutes, haggard, angry, jumpy.

She strode in to the center of the loft, ignoring the curious cats and looking around as if she had entered a tent in the Mongolian desert. Then she plopped down hard onto the sofa and began to remove items from her large briefcase.

"You don't know what I've been through, Alice. The funeral was bad enough . . . but this estate nonsense can drive you insane. Wills. No wills. Trustees. Attorneys. Judges. Brokers. Bankers. They're all as treacherous as snakes and greedy as honey bees."

I took a seat next to her. "Are you sure you wouldn't like some coffee or tea?"

In response, she slapped a thick packet of canceled checks, fastened with a rubber band, into my hand. "The New York lawyer found these. From a joint bank account."

I undid the rubber band and started to shuffle, confusedly, through the checks. What was I expected to do with them?

Gloria grabbed the packet back angrily and went through the papers, deftly removing checks from the pile here and there. "Now listen and look, Alice."

She pointed to one check in particular.

"See this one? Nothing really interesting here. One of his charitable donations to a hospital—for eighteen thousand dollars. Signed by him, Ivan Tasso. Most of the checks were. But not this one." And she pointed to another check, this one for $120, made out to a greengrocer on First Avenue, signed, this time, by Amanda.

I looked at her blankly. What was so unusual about a woman in an affluent neighborhood writing a check to the grocer's? I had no idea what Gloria was getting at. "So?"

"So nothing. Not peculiar at all, right?"

"Right," I agreed.

"But take a look at these!" she ordered. And she laid out three checks, one right next to the other.

The first was for $40,000.

The second for $55,000 dollars.

The third for $71,000 dollars.

This was serious money. All three checks were signed by Amanda and issued within the past year.

When I saw who they were made out to, I went pale, pale as the proverbial sheet.

But only for a few seconds. Then I felt a surge of intellectual triumph. Vindication! Sweet, blessed vindication.

I had been right. I smacked my hand down hard onto the checks.

"What's going on, Alice? Do you know this Red Lion Productions outfit? Can you tell me why Amanda gave them $166,000 dollars?"

"Oh, I surely do know them, Gloria. Would you like an introduction?"

"Of course I would."

"How about right now?"

This made the second time I had barged into the offices of Red Lion Productions. But this time I had Amanda's sister in tow, not Sam Tully (a "thug," Harvey had called him), and I was holding the three whopping checks in front of me like a spook hunter wielding a crucifix to deter a vampire.

The moment Joan Engel saw the checks, she froze.

"Good morning, Joan. May I introduce you to Gloria Avery," I said, grinning. "I wanted you to hear me when I told her how you and Harvey robbed Amanda of her money, then of her creative property, and finally her life."

My words seemed to set Gloria spinning. In disbelief, she looked first at me, then at Joan, then back to me.

"What are you saying, Alice?" All the brass was gone from her manner and her voice. She was soft-spoken, afraid.

Joan sat down heavily.

Still holding the checks, and shaking them like a baby's rattle from time to time, I told Gloria exactly what I thought had transpired.

I spoke simply, quickly, succinctly. My words, alas, beat a tattoo of horror upon Gloria Avery. Then my tale was finished. I stopped talking abruptly.

There we were, as Virginia Woolf would say. Three women in a room. Silent for the longest time. The air had become insufferably close.

"The police—call the police," Gloria finally choked out.

Joan Engel gave out with a theatrical moan. "Why is the world so full of idiots?" she asked, ever so wearily. "Idiots and basket cases. Don't listen to a thing this woman says, Miss Avery. It's common knowledge she's having a nervous breakdown. I guess I shouldn't be angry at her. She needs to be taken care of . . . looked after . . . medicated . . . something. But not ever listened to or taken seriously. Never!

"You really want to know what these checks are all about? I'll tell you. But—listen to me carefully—*I'm* telling this, not Miss Alice Nestleton. Do you understand? Because if you want to hear anything more from her, you can do it somewhere else. Understood?"

Neither Gloria nor I said a word.

Joan leaned forward and spoke in a hushed, intense voice. She addressed Gloria and Gloria alone.

"Amanda fell in love with Harvey Stith. She palled around with my nephew Lyle, but it was Harvey she was crazy over. The feelings were not reciprocated. Amanda pouted over it for a while, but she recovered. Harvey remained her friend, her good friend, and Amanda contented herself with that. She probably came to her senses and realized she could never cheat on her husband anyway.

"As time went on she became absolutely obsessed with jumpstarting Harvey's career. She got this crazy idea that she was going to create a hit show for him—a blockbuster musical based on the novel *Mrs. Dalloway*. She delivered the script and the songs to me. It was impossible—pathetically amateurish. I didn't want to hurt her feelings. I had to find some excuse for my lack of commitment to her project. So I told her that it was a bad time for musicals, that all the investors' money had dried up, I couldn't possibly find backers.

"That didn't work. She began giving me the money to do the show myself. I took the checks and then put all the money into a safe escrow account for her. It was my way of stalling. I just had to hope she would come to her senses one day and drop the idea. But of course she didn't—even after her husband died. Once the funeral was out of the way and she got back to living her life, she began pestering me again. Finally I decided I had to tell her the whole damn

105

truth—that *Mrs. Dalloway*, the musical, couldn't make it as a junior high school review, let alone a Broadway show. But before I had a chance to return the money to her—well, the tragedy happened; Amanda was murdered."

Joan suddenly began to open drawers in the desk, then to extract envelopes from the drawers and paper from one envelope in particular. "Here!" she said. "See for yourself."

She slid a bank statement across the desk to Gloria.

I could see it as well. Yes. Every cent of the money was intact. Yes, it was in an escrow account for Amada Avery.

Oh.

Well.

Hmmm.

Those were among the more intelligent one-syllable things it crossed my mind to say. I didn't say any of them, though.

I just slunk out of the Red Lion office, never looking back. So it was "common knowledge" that I was around the bend, eh?

Well, maybe so. Maybe that's why I began to hear that melody in my head. I rode down in the elevator humming to myself: *Gotta wash this case right outta my hair.*

It wasn't so hard to wash that case out of my life. But what about Jake and Good Girl? What about their case?

The cat had vanished. There was little I could do about that, particularly if he was indeed the feline Willie Sutton.

Good Girl was another story. She needed a home. I was tempted to call Gloria before she returned to Beloit and tell her I was resigning from the task. But I couldn't do it. I had the nagging suspicion that Gloria Avery would simply dump the helpless Good Girl at the nearest ASPCA facility.

As you can imagine, gloom descended on me.

I was losing my touch, it seemed, in every way. I'd been totally wrong about Stith and Engel and their plot to bilk Amanda, unable to find homes for Amanda's orphaned pets, and I'd let the strangely beautiful harlequin cat Jake get away from me.

When Tully called me the next day, he was in a gloom of his own.

"What's the matter with you?" he asked.

"What's the matter with *you*?" I retorted.

He didn't answer.

"Well, Tully, you remember my brilliant script detailing the ways and means of Amanda's murder."

"Yeah."

"It was sheer nonsense."

"Ouch. Bad break."

"And as for Jake . . ."

"He never turned up, huh?"

"No. But would you like to take a stab at the real story on that cat?"

"No."

"He's the namesake of a famous felon. In the trade, so

to speak, they call him Willie Sutton. Why? 'Cause no house can hold him."

"Who would've figured it, honey?"

Sam was quiet for a while, then he spoke: "I'll tell you what it is that's getting me down, Nestleton. This trying to make Harry Bondo sweet and gentle and wholesome."

"I imagine it must be difficult."

"Yeah. But I got the title at least: *Only Daisies Don't Die*."

"Well, Sam, it's kind of sweet. Cryptic but sweet."

"And I got some ideas about how poor old Harry makes the transition."

I had never heard Sam talk about his Bondo character that way, calling him "poor old Harry." It was often the way I thought about Sam. "That's good," was all I said.

"But, honey, I can sure use some help."

"The way I feel now, Sam, I don't think I'd be much help."

"Yeah, I know you're wiped out. Just half an hour, what do you say, Nestleton?"

How could I refuse him? "Where?" I asked resignedly.

"I'll make it easy for you. The White Horse on Hudson."

"Around noon?"

"Okay."

So there I was, once again in a bar with Sam Tully. At least the White Horse—a Village landmark tavern—had a touch of respectability and cheeriness, unlike his usual haunts. At least they served food along with the booze.

I arrived first, sat down at a table against the wall, and ordered a toasted English muffin and a club soda. They had no English muffins, the waitress told me. I took a grilled cheese sandwich instead.

Sam came in and immediately ordered his usual poison. But he didn't even taste the drink when it arrived; he got right to the point.

"Let me lay out the problem for you, Nestleton."

"I'm listening."

"A Harry Bondo mystery hasn't been published in a while. But I got a whole lot of readers out there—Bondo fans. So if and when *Only Daisies Don't Die* comes out, what the hell are these people going to think? It's a betrayal, honey! They're going to ask: Who's this clown? He sure isn't the nitty-gritty, boozing, around-the-bend, skirt-chasing philosopher they've come to love."

"Yes, I understand the problem, Sam."

"The only way I can think of doing it is . . . well . . . in the opening chapter of the new book he's the same old Harry. But then, in the second chapter, something real bad happens to him, and he has a spiritual crisis."

Sam took a sip of his poison.

"What do you think, honey?"

"It seems to make sense. But are you talking about a religious conversion? Something like that?"

"Yeah. Something like that."

And then his face broke into a huge grin.

"What's so funny?"

"I have to level with you, honey."

"By all means."

"I didn't get you here to talk about Harry Bondo."

"Then why? What's the mystery, Sam?"

"No mystery. I just decided to give it a try."

"Give what a try? Come on, Tully, stop being so coy."

"The dog."

"Dog?"

"Good Girl, you know," he said sheepishly.

I almost leaped across the table and hugged him. "That's wonderful, Tully! Absolutely wonderful!"

"But listen, Nestleton, if Pickles tries to eat that hound—and you know about leopards, I warned you—then the thing is called off."

It was obvious, when they met, that Sam and Good Girl had hit it off. But Sam adopting her? Not in my wildest dreams.

I didn't want to hear any more, and given the circumstances, I surely wasn't interested in the grilled cheese sandwich.

"Go home, Sam. I'll be there with Good Girl in an hour."

I rushed out, caught a cab, and went to Amanda's apartment. I leashed Good Girl, gathered up her bowl and several cans of dog food, and rushed back downtown.

Sam was waiting for me just outside the door of his apartment.

"Remember, honey," he warned, "if Pickles goes for her we gotta be there. We have to stay sharp. Like I said, you can't figure a leopard. He may see a meal, he may see a friend. Hell, he might even see a sofa. But believe me, when Pickles moves, he moves fast."

Then he started scratching Good Girl's head. "You a sofa?" he asked her.

We went inside. The windows onto the fire escape were open. I knew what that meant.

"Winter's here, Sam. You still going to let Pickles wander in and out like that? Soon there'll be ice all over those fire escapes and on the ledges. He's just a house cat, after all."

"Ice means nothing to leopards, honey. Pickles likes the fire escape. He likes the roof. I hang out in bars, he hangs out on roofs. To each his own."

I unleashed Good Girl, who began inspecting the premises in her leisurely fashion.

"I don't think there'll be any trouble, Sam. She likes cats. At least, she liked Jake—and he was hardly Mr. Friendly. He tolerated her, anyway."

"Pickles is a whole different ball game. He's no Willie Sutton. He don't vanish."

Good Girl stopped her ambling and stared up adoringly at Sam. He gently tugged on one of her massive ears.

A startling face suddenly appeared at the window. No matter how many times you see Pickles, he frightens you a bit each time. Nor does it matter if you already know he's just a normal kind of Bengal cat—although it's a fairly new breed—because he really does look and move like a miniature leopard, from the eyes to the spots to the color to the shape of his limbs.

Pickles did not enter the apartment. He just stood with his back legs on the fire escape, his front paws on the windowsill, and eyed Good Girl.

Finally the big dog noticed him. She plopped down and began wagging her long tail happily, beating out a message with it on Sam's crumbling wood floor.

Pickles vanished for a few seconds, then peered in again. He repeated the procedure.

"He's going to make a move," Sam whispered, tense.

"Take it easy, Sam. Everything's going to be okay," I answered, but I had to admit my reassurances were a bit tentative.

Pickles suddenly leapt inside and stood absolutely still where he had landed.

The dog yelped delightedly, got to her feet, shook herself, and headed toward her new friend.

Pickles snapped into attack mode—hissing, lips curled, hair standing on end, ears forward. Making matters worse was the fact that he did not arch his back like a normal house cat but hunkered down low, like a hunting leopard on a tree limb.

Good Girl, perplexed, stopped in her tracks. Then, a blur of spotted yellow limbs! Pickles zoomed past her to the apartment door across the room. He sat back on his haunches and began emitting long, rather pitiful meows.

Then there occurred one of the most bizarre turns of events I have ever witnessed. Good Girl lumbered over to the window with great huffing and puffing, and actually climbed out of it and onto the fire escape. Pickles shot back over to the window and stared out at the dog. In a minute, Good Girl climbed back in—and Pickles leaped lightly out. We were back to square one!

Good Girl lifted her head and gave out the most mournful howl I have ever heard.

"I thought Gordon setters were bird dogs," Sam said. "My God! She sounds like a wolf."

We tried to quiet her, but it was no good. She went on howling. Pickles jumped through the window again, this time landing only two feet from the yapping setter. I moved quickly between them to forestall bloodshed.

But all Pickles did was sit down, stare curiously at Good Girl, and then calmly begin to clean his right paw with his tongue.

"Home free!" Sam cried in triumph.

I knew in my heart he was absolutely right. Good Girl had stopped making that infernal racket. She lay peacefully near her feline brother, sound asleep.

I danced down the shaky stairwell and out of Tully's old

tenement. My losing streak had ended—not just ended—I had hit the jackpot. I was so proud and happy. Good Girl had a home.

I was a long way from being flush, gambling metaphors to the contrary. So I had to content myself with mere window shopping instead of the real thing. Up and down Spring Street I walked, reveling, fantasizing about all those chic black dresses and hats in the boutiques that seemed to sprout like mushrooms and then vanish before you could save enough money to make a purchase.

It was a beautiful, sunny if cold day. I realized I was underdressed. But for the moment, I didn't care. I hadn't felt this good in weeks.

I was hungry. At the corner of Spring and Broadway, I stopped in a cafe and had tuna salad on a croissant and apple juice. Tasty—but not enough mayo, I thought as I ate avidly. I began to laugh out loud. From the looks they were sending my way, the young couple seated next to me at the cheery counter must have thought I was quite mad. Well, it was common knowledge, wasn't it? I laughed even harder.

I looked through the cafe window. Across the street was a bank, and in front of it was a newly installed pay phone, so new in fact that it gleamed in the midday sun. It wouldn't stay that way for long. I dashed out to use it before the first vandal could get his hands on it. I dialed up my true love, Anthony Basillio.

He was, predictably, still in bed. His answering machine

kicked in, and I only had time to say, "Hi, Tony," before he picked up. "You must have the wrong number, lady," he said nastily. "This is Con Edison."

"Come now, Tony," I answered placatingly. "Don't be like that. I miss you."

"Sorry, lady. I think you're mixing me up with somebody you have a relationship with."

"Oh, Tony. You know how life can get when there are so many things cluttering it up."

"*Cluttering!*" he shouted. And I think he used a very impolite four-letter word as well.

But not even that could dissuade me from my good mood. I understood: the poor guy loved me, and I had been avoiding him.

"I am going to make amends, Basillio," I announced.

"Oh, is that so?" His tone was still hostile, but I knew he was interested now.

"I'm making you a special meat loaf tonight. And mashed potatoes just the way you like them—with light cream and garlic. And green peas I'm going to shell with my own lily-white hands. But wait—no, no—you don't like fresh, wholesome peas, do you? You prefer the canned variety. I'll get those. How does that sound? What other busy girl would pamper you like that, Tony? After all, you're a handsome devil, but you're also an out-of-work bum."

Finally, I had made him laugh. "What's for dessert?" he asked.

"What would you like?"

"You know what I'd like."

"You are a lewd man, Basillio."

"What time do you want me?"

"About seven. Will you be staying?"

"Only eight or nine days."

"Ha-ha. What about Tiny and Tim?"

"I'll hire a cat-sitter."

"Not too funny. Tony, listen, Sam Tully has adopted Good Girl."

"No kidding? It's about time that old drunk did something for his country. What about that nutty-looking cat?"

"Gone."

"Gone where?"

"We don't know. He escaped. Just ran off. He's some sort of sociopath, Tony. They call him Willie Sutton. He escapes from penitentiaries and such."

"That's nice. You want me to bring anything tonight?"

"Wine."

"I shall bring you a case."

"Sure, Tony. A case of red and a case of white. And maybe a few bottles of some Scottish ale so dark that it's black . . . and maybe a script with a great part for me . . . and some pearl earrings."

"Are you okay, Swede? You been smoking something funny?"

"Tony, did you ever, as the old people used to say, feel like a million bucks?"

"Once. I was seven."

I stared across the street at the little restaurant where only a few minutes ago I'd eaten a tuna sandwich with not quite enough mayonnaise. My seat at the counter had not yet been taken. But the couple who had witnessed my laughing fit were still there, and they seemed to be peering out the window at me, as if watching my progress. I waved to them merrily. And, after a few hesitating seconds, they waved back.

"Alice!" I heard Tony calling into the receiver. "Hey, where are you?"

"I'm here, Tony! I'm here . . . and there . . . and everywhere! Know what I am, Tony? I'm written on the wind."

"Wow! You *are* in a good mood, aren't you. Just hang in there till seven tonight, okay?"

"Okay, see you," I said, and hung up. I threw another wave at the couple across the street and began the walk home.

As every glorious high, every winning streak must, mine came to an abrupt end. It happened when I turned into my street and spotted the ugly gas guzzler of a car parked in front of my loft building. In a split second, all that happiness was gone.

The NYPD was back in my life.

117

Chapter 9

"Join us, Miss Nestleton?" Detective Webster said. It was not the polite invitation it might have been had someone else spoken those words. In fact, there was a distinct air of menace in the words.

I went into the back seat of the vehicle feeling almost as though it were the chariot of death.

Behind the wheel, Detective Luboff barely acknowledged me at all.

"We haven't heard from you," Yvonne Webster stated, turning in her seat to face me. I caught sight of a frilly white collar under her coat. Apparently she had forsworn the *Cagney and Lacey* look (dark trousers and blazer) in favor of something more like a schoolmarm in an old western.

"No, you haven't heard from me," I affirmed. "That's because I had nothing to report."

"Nothing else you remember about that night?"

"No."

"Nothing more about Amanda Avery's friends?"

"No."

"Nothing about your friend Basillio?"

"I remember many things about my friend Tony, Detective. But they have nothing to do with this case."

"So," Detective Luboff spoke languidly, "you got nothing about nothing for us."

"That's correct."

"Tell me, Miss Nestleton," Webster said, "how do you like the color green? You're a blonde; blondes look pretty good in that color. What do you think of it?"

I couldn't even imagine where she was going with this line of questioning, so I took the seemingly absurd question at face value. "Green is nice," I said.

"You wear much of it yourself?"

"Not much. When I was young, maybe. But not anymore. I have a pretty simple wardrobe now that I'm older."

"Isn't it funny how both dark women and fair women both like green, Miss Nestleton? I guess it just depends on the shade of green."

I didn't know how to answer that inane observation, and so I did not try.

"You own a green cloak with a hood, Miss Nestleton?"

119

"I do not."

"Did you ever have one?"

"No."

"We have a description now of a woman in the vicinity of the murder, at about the time of death. A man walking his dog saw a woman wearing a green cloak-type garment with a hood. The description wasn't very detailed, but it could have been you."

"That may be true," I said testily. "But even if I had such a cloak, you know exactly where I was before, during, and after Amanda's murder—with Harvey Stith. We were following in Amanda's tracks. And, if I had been wearing a coat like that, surely the arriving EMS people—and the police—would have noticed it. But I'm sure you've already asked them."

"You could have dumped the coat," Luboff barked.

"Yes, I suppose so—*if* I had one and *if* I was wearing one and *if* I could be in two places at once. But you haven't found my cloak, have you? No. And I'll tell you why: because I didn't wear it, I didn't dump it, and I didn't kill Amanda."

As infuriating as it was to be suspected of kidnapping and murder, I still retained a little pity for Detective Webster. It crossed my mind to tell her that I too had followed a really stupid line of investigation when I was convinced that Harvey and Joan had been responsible for Amanda's death. But I kept my mouth shut about that.

Detective Webster was talking again. "Our dog walker saw something else. The woman in the green cloak stopped to wash her hands at a dripping fire hydrant on Eleventh Avenue."

"You mean she was washing away the blood, literally? Or a Pontius Pilate scenario?"

"We don't know for sure the woman was involved in the Avery murder."

"But you think she was."

"Yes," she said petulantly.

I was really beginning to feel sorry for Yvonne Webster. The case was going nowhere. No wonder she and Luboff were getting desperate. I leaned back on the seat, a bit less defensive now.

A woman in a hooded green cape. Washing her hands. Most peculiar.

"I don't think it was her," I announced suddenly.

Detective Webster was caught off guard. "Who?" she asked.

"The woman in green. Whoever she was. I don't think she killed Amanda."

"Oh? Why not?"

"Well, think about it, Detective Webster. Wouldn't it take a great deal of strength to drive an ice pick so deep into a person's back? To kill so efficiently?"

"You mean you think it was a man?"

"It makes more sense," I replied.

"But it wasn't an ice pick." It was the taciturn Luboff who added that information.

I looked up, startled by his remark.

"That's right," said Webster. "It turns out the weapon was one of those long, thin screwdrivers with prongs. Used a lot in electronic repairs. And there was a funny residue on the weapon. A kind of lint or fuzz. We're figuring the killer was wearing thick leather gloves with some kind of fuzzy lining."

"I don't know what to make of that," I admitted. I guess that was the wrong thing to have said, because Webster suddenly burst into sardonic laughter.

"You know, Miss Nestleton," she said, "you're talking like we're here to consult you. Like you're taking time out of your busy schedule to help us clear up this case. Let me tell you something, miss. We know a thing or two about you. Oh, yeah, we heard the rumors about you and the Department. They call you the cat lady because you once helped the Department out with some loonies who were going around killing people with cats—or whatever that crazy case was. But get this straight: We do not need your guidance to clear this case. We just need you to jog your memory a bit—and to come clean about what you know. Is that understood?"

"Whatever you say, Detective Webster." I knew when I was licked.

A minute later I was dismissed.

What a roller coaster of a day. I wanted off. If a police grilling was the price I had to pay for the kind of wild high I'd known earlier in the day, I'd have to choose the middle ground—neither high nor low. I went upstairs and took a nap.

About four in the afternoon, feeling refreshed, I went shopping for Tony's dinner. First I walked into the heart of the Village, to the Jefferson Market on Sixth Avenue, to obtain two pounds of their special meat loaf mixture, already blended, spiced, shaped, and ready to pop into the oven.

Next, the supermarket, where I picked up two cans of Green Giant Leseur peas—Tony's inexplicable favorite. The potatoes I already had in the pantry. Tony liked it when I mixed three different varieties—red skin, Idaho, and Yukon Gold—for his mashed potatoes. If milk chocolate, Fritos, and Häagen-Dazs ice cream were the preferred balms for depressed women, mashed potatoes seemed to be the comfort food of choice for men.

Back in the loft, I began my preparations under the careful scrutiny of Bushy and Pancho, who were always warily curious when I put on that green canvas apron. I think they were probably still living with the memory of that mince pie disaster we'd had many years ago in the old apartment.

"Not a word out of either of you," I warned them as I lit the stove, "or you'll be on dry food and water for the next month."

Tony was due at seven. But I knew him and his ways. He'd never arrived anywhere exactly on time in his life. He was invariably either early or late. Therefore it was no surprise to me when his knock at the apartment door came at five minutes to six. He was laden with gifts—white wine, red wine, cold beer, warm beer, and a truckload of pretty yellow irises.

He wanted to make love before dinner. I restrained him. But he didn't sulk more than a few minutes. I teased him and he yelled at me a bit, but it was all in fun. We were having a good time.

Back together again. That was, for better or worse, the nature of our affair . . . our friendship . . . our, to use *that* word, relationship. Together. Fighting. Apart. Making up. On again. Off again. Like a dance to an ever-changing beat, but always with the same steps. It could be a frustrating relationship, but after all these years, I'd accepted it. We loved each other, after a fashion.

And, of course, the one thing we had always loved—without reservations or argument—was the theater. It was the thing that kept us going, although, to be honest, neither of us really knew what the word meant anymore, since we worked so seldom.

As for the sex . . . well, it was good when it occurred. But it always fell a little short of what someone had once called "blessed eros." There was always a bit of sadness in bed with us because I believed Basillio to be an incurable philanderer and he believed that I really longed not for him but for some stage Galahad—perhaps Olivier, may he rest in peace.

It was a "fine meal," Tony declared. He was eating like there was no tomorrow. He consumed three-quarters of the meat loaf, an entire can of peas, and all of the potatoes, as I had declined to share the calories.

While he gorged, I filled him in on my recent adventures and misadventures connected with Amanda, her sister, her friends, and her animals.

"Are you sure that old idiot Tully can take care of a geriatric dog as well as a cat? If I recall, you told me he lets his cat go in and out of the window whenever it wants to—and up to the roof even. If he treats Eggplant that way, what the hell is he going to do with this dog?"

"The cat's name isn't Eggplant, Tony. It's Pickles. And look, I know you and Sam don't get along so well, but give the man credit where credit is due. He's got a fourteen-carat heart."

"Delusion, Swede. You're dreaming, as usual. His heart isn't made of diamonds. It's all Wild Turkey."

I got up from the table in disgust and made coffee.

Tony was fascinated with Jake's story, particularly his nom de guerre—Willie Sutton.

He sipped his coffee and reminisced expansively. "I remember hearing about Willie Sutton when I was a kid. And then I saw his picture in the paper. I couldn't believe it. The feared bank robber and escape artist looked like the kindest, most frail little drugstore clerk."

"Well, I don't know that I'd call Jake the kindest cat I've ever known, but he certainly doesn't bother anybody. He's pretty small and mild-mannered. I guess it's that two-toned coat of his that disarms people—and his 'comedy/tragedy' kind of face. That coat *is* wild."

Tony laughed. "And his MO. What was it the guy from Queens told you? About the way he gets out most of the time?"

"The 'shadow trick,' he called it, or something close to that."

"Actually, I think they should call him the Harlequin-Shadow instead of Willie Sutton. It's more intense. Like a Marvel Comics character."

"I don't think Jake cares what he's called."

"Hey, did you ever think maybe Jake taught Good Girl that shadow trick?"

"Impossible. She's too large, too old, and too slow to pull it off."

"See? You're delusional again. If Tully had enough booze in him, an arthritic hippo could slip past him."

"Oh, shut up, Tony."

We drank more wine and listened to music for a while. We went to bed early and made love as though we were young again. You know, there was even a kind of lovely desperation to it.

I woke suddenly, sat up, a gasp in my throat.
It was 3:15 A.M.

What had awakened me? The cats playing with their toys? Tony snoring? Revelers outside? A terrible dream?

I looked about. Tony, of the tousled salt-and-pepper hair, was soundlessly fast asleep. Bushy was also sleeping; he had made his bed on the window ledge rather than beside me. He rarely intruded on my privacy when there was another man in the house. Pancho was awake. I could see his glowing eyes over at the far end of the loft, but he wasn't making a sound.

How strange, to be awakened that way and not know why. I just knew I was markedly uncomfortable. Anxious. Maybe even plain old depressed.

Why? Was it Jake? Was I worried about where he was and what he was doing? Was I frightened that he had exhausted his proverbial nine lives?

No. It wasn't the fate of the harlequin cat that was worrying me. For some reason I had the feeling that wherever he was, Willie Sutton was okay.

It wasn't the recent erotic adventure with Basillio, I knew. That was great. It felt good to be close to Tony again. But maybe it was just a case of *omni animale post coitu triste*—the inevitable depression that descends on all creatures after sex.

That speculation made me smile. My first serious acting teacher, at the Guthrie, used to say that the same aphorism applies to the theater: actors feel that same letdown, the same depression, after a great performance.

I got out of bed quietly, put on a robe, and went to the kitchen area to make a cup of tea. The light from the street-lamps flooded through the window, throwing a long thin core of illumination across the center of the loft, as if some-one had painted a stripe on the air.

By the time I had the kettle on, Bushy was off the ledge. He was a bit confused, wondering, I suppose, whether he should start screeching for his breakfast, although his body clock told him otherwise.

Pancho came to life, too, and started one of his desper-ate runs from unseen stalkers. He was being noisier than usual, his claws like bouncing marbles on the loft floor. I realized it was time to cut his nails—and Bushy's. I used to do it myself, sneaking up on them with the clippers while they dozed—and *wham!* But for a while now, I'd been tak-ing them in either to the cat groomer or the vet. It was a luxury I could now afford because I had so little rent to pay.

Wouldn't you know—these days it was the deranged Pancho who now climbed into his carrier without a com-plaint when it was time to visit the vet. Preening old Bushy had to be wrestled in.

I watched the rising steam as the kettle began to boil, dropping a tea bag into my large blue cup, the one with the stand of willows etched into the glaze.

Bushy came a little closer.

"No way, buster! You had it right the first time. No breakfast yet."

He sat down and stared defiantly at me. I stared back. It was his favorite game.

"I'm telling you right now," I warned, "you are going to the vet soon for those nails. And if you give me any trouble this time, I'll . . . I'll bring you to grief. Hear me, buster?"

He never broke his gaze. I smiled at him. He won that one.

I poured the tea and went to one of the window ledges to drink it. Bushy followed and climbed up beside me. I looked down onto the street. Nobody and nothing down there. A few blackened leaves in the gutter, holdovers from the fall shedding, mixed with assorted flotsam, all blown about by the night wind. Yes, winter was creeping up on the city.

Pancho, worn out by his labors, ambled by to see what was happening in the rational world. "I'll tell you, too, Panch. If you so much as blink when I'm taking you in to get clipped, you're going to end up like Maybelline."

Poor Maybelline. What a story. It had been a long time since I thought of Inez Miller and her cat Maybelline. I did cat-sitting for her often.

Then Inez moved out of the city, upstate somewhere. On the day of the move, I went over just to help out. Moving is always such a traumatic event, and Inez was a nervous sort. But there was nothing much for me to do. Inez had hired an outfit that took care of everything. The two of us sat around and chatted while the movers boxed everything and then loaded the van.

Soon there was nothing left in the apartment—nothing, that is, other than Maybelline. Inez said good-bye to me and went after the cat to put her into the carrier.

Now, Maybelline was the most charming and ladylike of cats. But on that day, at that moment, in those circumstances—she flipped.

I mean, *flipped*. She fought like a tiger. She screeched. She clawed. She hissed. She bit. We could do nothing with her.

Inez became frantic. The movers didn't want to wait any longer; they had a schedule. They began to threaten Inez with enormous overtime charges. So Inez phoned one of those veterinary emergency lines. Twenty minutes later a young woman vet showed up. She took one look at Maybelline, who was crouched and hissing in the bathtub, and promptly pulled on a massive pair of gloves that made her look as if she was going to joust in a medieval tournament.

"Wait here," the vet ordered us. Then she walked into the bathroom and shut the door behind her. We heard the sounds of a battle royal. Poor Inez was in tears.

At last, out they came. Maybelline was once again the lovely, fluffy, well-mannered lady, and she was happily ensconced in the stranger's arms.

Of course, the lady vet, whose name was Francesca, had given Maybelline a sedative—a shot in the rump.

I waggled a finger at both of my kitties and told them: "Yes, you had better remember what happened to Maybelline." I could only hope they were more frightened than they appeared, that their yawns of boredom were just a brave front.

I took another sip of my tea and decided a little sugar would be nice. I stood up and headed toward the kitchen.

But I stopped in my tracks after only two steps. Something was nagging at me ferociously.

Those gloves! The animal handler gloves the young vet had used to restrain Maybelline. What were they made of? Leather!

What had Detective Webster said? The murderer had worn leather gloves.

Why? As a precaution—in case Jake acted up?

I walked quickly back to the window ledge and sat down. My head was spinning. There were beads of sweat on my forehead.

The woman in the green cloak had washed her hands at a dripping hydrant. She had taken off her cat-restraining gloves and washed her hands. Was that because she had blood on her hands? Was it symbolic? Was it just nerves?

The gloves! The washing of hands!

These were simply facts hitting me on the head. They were somehow familiar. As if I had played the scene before.

My God! I stood straight up and gave one of those silly little shouts. Not too loud—like a Girl Scout having made a whopping big cookie sale.

Abide! The animal shelter where Amanda and I had

found Jake. The signs at Abide. There were signs all over the place. Wash your hands after handling any cat. Wash your hands!

And the murder weapon. What had the detectives said about it? The weapon was not an ice pick. It was a long, thin, pronged screwdriver. Luboff said it was a tool often used in electronics repair.

I didn't know anything about that, but I did know for sure that such tools were used to assemble and disassemble the steel cages and kennels where the animals in shelters were kept.

I looked around for some kind of help, some kind of affirmation. Because it was now clear to me that the kidnapping of Jake and the murder of Amanda Avery had originated at the animal shelter known as Abide.

Chapter 10

I'm no rocket scientist, as the saying goes. But I am a woman who can follow a series of markers to the end of the trail—whether said markers are simply notches cut into the trees or pieces of colored cloth dropped onto the ground every twenty yards.

I now knew where the markers led. But it took me two hours to figure out what to do next.

And when I did figure it out, there was the inescapable fact that the services of one Tony Basillio were required.

That is why, at five-twenty in the morning, I was seated on the bed beside the sleeping Tony, deciding how best to wake him.

Bushy jumped up also, and together we studied the sleeping terrestrial. After careful deliberation I decided on the left foot, which was brazenly thrust out from the blanket. I pulled aggressively on the two largest toes.

He awoke with a start. "What's the matter!" He looked around wildly, frightening Bushy, who left quickly for parts unknown.

"Nothing's the matter," I said. "I just want to talk to you."

Tony's eyes found the illuminated dial of the clock radio.

"It's five-thirty in the morning. Are you nuts?"

"What are you doing today?"

"How the hell should I know? I'm not awake yet."

"I mean, are you looking for work?"

He laughed derisively. "I always look for work. That's what forty-year-old stage designers do, Madam Nestleton."

"But nothing's imminent, right?"

"You got it."

"I want you to volunteer your services, Tony."

"What are you talking about?"

"I want you to go to Abide."

"The shelter where you got Jake?"

"That's right."

"Why?"

"There were three volunteers in the cat adoption section on the day we took Jake. I've forgotten their names. One of them murdered Amanda."

"And how do you know that?"

I told him how I had put the puzzle together. How a sudden memory of a cat named Maybelline and her travails had set me on a most intriguing path.

When I finished, he swung his legs over the side of the bed and sank his head into his hands and groaned. At last he looked up. "What am I supposed to be doing there?"

"Find out their names, for starters. Socialize. Find out everything you can about them."

"I don't like this, Swede."

"It'll be good for you, Tony. A kind of vacation."

"Why don't we discuss this at a more reasonable hour?"

"Now."

"Okay. But I have some doubts about your brilliant analysis."

"The pieces fit, Tony: the gloves, the washing of hands, the weapon, the signs on the walls. Everything points back to the shelter where we picked up Jake. It all *fits*."

He was silent for a long while.

"Well?" I asked impatiently.

He leaned forward and kissed me on the cheek, in an almost brotherly fashion, then said, "What I am about to say, Swede, I don't want you to take the wrong way."

"Do I ever, Tony?"

"Always. But at any rate, let me make a point. You wake me up at five in the morning—okay, five-thirty. You are trying to send me out on a wild goose chase. Fine. This kind of thing is nothing new. However, it is obvious that you've been under a lot of tension lately. All kinds of things going on." He smiled gently. "To get to the point, you're acting peculiar."

"How so?"

"Well, for one, you've suddenly started talking in a modified upper-class Brit accent."

"Nonsense."

"See what I mean? 'Nonsense!' you said. You sound like Margaret Rutherford. Something peculiar is going on."

I didn't know how to respond. Was I, in some inexplicable way, aping Amanda Avery? Was I absconding with a piece of her Virginia Woolf dissertation? If so, why was I doing it? Did I really feel, deep down, that I was some sort of character from *Mrs. Dalloway*?

"Look, Tony," I finally said, "I'm an actress. I slip in and out of dialects. It's *Lady Windermere's Fan* this time . . . maybe. Besides, what do my linguistic peculiarities have to do with the price of tea in China?"

"At five in the morning, everything affects the price of tea."

"I'm asking you a favor, Tony. I shouldn't have to ask you twice. I shouldn't have to defend my request."

"No, you shouldn't. After all, we are lovers."

"Exactly."

"And longtime companions."

"Yes."

"And theatrical comrades in arms."

"Of course."

He lay back on his pillow. "So how can I refuse? Wake me at eight."

I woke him at seven-thirty. I made him medium-boiled eggs, rye toast with butter and jam, and coffee.

We left the loft at nine and proceeded to Tony's Twenty-sixth Street apartment, where we fed his Siamese cats, Tiny and Tim.

Then we took the First Avenue bus up to Thirty-fourth Street and walked the five blocks to Abide's street.

At the corner I gave Tony final instructions, which were really quite simple: "Walk in! Volunteer! Appear concerned! Accept all hours and all assignments! Keep your wisecracks to a minimum!"

"That's all?"

"Yes."

There was a gourmet shop/deli at Thirty-seventh and First, with outdoor tables. I would wait for him there, I said, no matter what happened. If they put him to work immediately, all he had to do was slip out for a minute and give me a report.

I watched him walk to the entrance. He turned and waved, then disappeared inside.

I went into the shop to buy a container of tea and then nursed it at one of the windswept outdoor tables. No doubt they'd bring these tables inside when the first snow hit.

I thought the wait would be measured in minutes: Tony would go in, sign up as a volunteer, and then leave with instructions as to when to return for his first labors. But twenty minutes passed without an appearance by Tony. Forty minutes. An hour.

I waited an hour and thirty-five minutes and was just about to go back downtown when I saw him approaching.

He was pulling—and being pulled by—a large, goofy-looking sheepdog-type beast on a thick leash.

"This is Harold," Tony announced, fighting to keep the dog in check. "It seems, Swede, that you didn't take into account that there is a dog section at Abide. They need volunteers desperately. Harold is my first assignment. I told them that I'd prefer to work with felines. They promised me I'd get my wish in due time, but right now, dog walkers were urgently needed."

Harold jammed his nose into my cold tea.

"So what now, boss?" Tony asked wearily.

"Persevere. Do your job. Visit the cat section when you get the chance. Hang around there. Get me the names of the three daytime volunteers who work inside the cat cage area. Use your charm, Tony. We all know you can turn it on."

He nodded grimly and allowed himself to be dragged off by Harold.

I didn't go straight home. I dropped in at Sam Tully's place to see how Good Girl and Pickles were getting along.

I found Sam at his ridiculous old manual typewriter, which, when a key was hit, thunked like an iron bolt being dropped onto a pail of mud.

"I am in the midst of poor Harry Bondo's spiritual crisis," he shouted, and then went back to ignoring me.

Pickles was not in sight, but the windows were open, so he obviously had gone up to his usual lair on the roof.

As for Good Girl, she was curled up on a tattered easy chair, her large frame hanging over the sides like a black and tan beach bag.

"Is everyone getting along, Sam?"

"Like three peas in a pod."

Then he ripped the sheet of paper out of the machine, added it to another pile of papers, rolled them up, and waved the package furiously. "I'm hot as a pistol," he exclaimed. "I'm going on all ten cylinders."

"That's nice. What are you talking about?"

"The book, honey, the book!"

"Oh, you mean *Only Daisies Don't Die*."

"Yeah. The transformation of Harry Bondo."

"It's going well, then?"

"Well? That is a wild understatement. I'm boiling, baby. Remember when I told you what I was doing?"

"Vaguely, Sam. A typical first chapter, you said. Then I think you used the term 'boom' and Harry has a religious conversion and turns into a combination of Father Brown and Francis of Assisi."

Lydia Adamson

"There's been a few changes since then—but I got the nut."

"The nut?"

"You know. The center of the plot. The meat. The ham what am. The core. The gist. The—"

"Yes, Sam. I understand what you mean."

"I won't read it to you now, but let me give you a taste."

"Sure."

He rushed into what could be called a kitchen and came back with a large glass of V8. He offered me a sip. I declined. He poured some Wild Turkey into the juice. A sickening combination.

"I've been discussing a lot of this with her," he said, nodding at the dog. "She's a helluva listener. Pickles, on the other hand, don't want to hear a thing from me. Not a word."

"Cats will be cats," I noted.

"Okay. Listen good. I'll just cover the major points. In the first chapter an old friend of Harry's, a lady of the night called Wanda, is found chopped up and the parts distributed in the subbasement of the Chrysler Building. The cops don't have a clue.

"So Harry pays a visit to her Korean pimp in Flushing: one Big Kim. It gets nasty. Harry knocks him around. Two bodyguards show up and do a number on Harry, then throw him down the stairs. Bondo takes a cab back to Manhattan and has a few drinks in a downtown bar. He's hurting. He has a few more. He ends up wandering around Chinatown."

140

Sam paused there, drained his concoction, lit a cigarette, and squinted. "You with me so far, Nestleton?"

"Yes, I'm following."

He turned to Good Girl. "You with me, doll?"

There was a slight movement of her tail, very slight.

"Okay. Now we get close to the bone, honey. So there's Bondo, bruised, drunk, ugly, depressed, wandering the streets of Chinatown. He stops in front of a food store and lights a cigarette. Then he looks . . . *up.*"

Sam stopped his summary for a moment, dropped his voice to a dramatic whisper, and raised his right hand in an expansive gesture. "Yeah," he continued, "he looks up, high up, and sees ducks hanging on a rail. Now, anyone who walks around Chinatown sooner or later sees whole barbecued ducks hung by their necks in the window of a shop—beak and head still intact.

"It's a sight Bondo has seen a hundred times. Sometimes there're twelve or thirteen ducks and sometimes there're only a couple of them. But there's something about the number of ducks this time—Harry never saw *seven* in a row like that before.

"He steps back. It's like he's been kicked in the head. Why? Because he's remembering—he's remembering a photo. It was one of the most famous photos from World War Two. Seven Soviet partisans hung by the SS in the Ukraine. Three of them women. One just a boy. There are signs around their necks. And they're all hanging from the gibbet—never cut down—side by side—heads twisted in death. Oh, it is a photo of terrible ugliness.

"Bondo looks up at the window again. And suddenly, as if a divine light has cut through the night air—whoosh! Right there, he has the revelation."

Tully smiled and waited for me to speak.

"What? What?" I asked. "What is the revelation?"

"He becomes a vegetarian."

All I could do was sit there in stunned silence. How do you respond to a story like that? Laughter was highly inappropriate . . . wasn't it?

"Well, doll? What's the matter? Don't you see?"

"Uh—"

"Think about it," Tully insisted. "Just by becoming a vegetarian in his heart, he becomes a kinder, gentler Harry Bondo. Not much else is needed. Boom! There he is! See? Get it?"

"Sam, I don't want to rain on your parade, but there was a gentleman named Adolf Hitler who was a vegetarian."

"Don't bother me with stuff like that, Nestleton."

"But Sam—"

"The man has become a vegetarian. He'll never eat a barbecued duck again. Don't you see the symbolism?"

"Well, I guess you do have a point. Good luck with the rest of the book. I have to go now."

Sam fired another sheet of paper into the machine.

A CAT OF ONE'S OWN

That afternoon, while waiting for Tony to check in, I started going through my clothes.

Don't ask me why. I just suddenly felt the urge to conduct a major clothes-culling session.

I set up several large shopping bags outside my one huge closet. One bag was for clothes destined for the Salvation Army thrift shop, either because they were in bad shape or because they had been serious shopping mistakes or because I had simply grown to hate them.

A second bag was for those things I still liked but could not currently wear until they were altered. Yes, I had put on a few pounds, and taking them off was proving a lot harder than finding a decent tailor.

Another bag was for garments that were still in respectable condition, but that I was too old to wear. Nice legs aside, I didn't want to be one of those women who try to look younger by wearing things you'd expect to see on a high school senior's back.

The final bag was for clothes that had to be considered and reconsidered. That is, I had to think carefully before deciding whether they went into bag one, bag two, bag three, or back on the hanger.

As I said, the closet—the only one in the loft—was huge. When the place had been an industrial space, this closet was the men's room. But despite its size, it was filled to bursting. Not because I'm a clotheshorse. (In fact, a number of people I knew thought I dressed like a dork, as one of my friend's daughters put it.)

No, I am decidedly not a clothes fanatic. The reason for all the stuff in there is simple: I have a big problem getting rid of things. It's a trait I inherited from my grandmother. But of course I am nowhere near as bad as she was.

Like most farm women, Gram saved everything—broken spoons, string, eggshells, spent lightbulbs, and so on. I wouldn't have been surprised to find embalmed woodchucks in the cellar of her house. But clothes were the worst. They were inviolable, as if once you bought a garment it was yours for life.

If my grandmother had a pair of winter gloves, for example, and those gloves were burned in a barn fire, soaked in cow urine, shredded by a threshing machine, dipped in rat poison, and finally pulverized by a mulcher—she would still save them, even if it meant keeping the pieces in a plastic sandwich bag. She'd be absolutely shocked at the suggestion that they should be discarded. Clean them? Of course. Mend them? Yes. But give up on them, throw them away? Never!

I filled my shopping bags slowly, giving each garment the deliberation due it. Bushy, and to a lesser degree Pancho, seemed mighty interested in my movements. From time to time I gave them explanations for my choice of bags. I even slipped on and modeled for them a couple of garments that were really close calls.

The six p.m. telephone call from Tony brought me back

to reality. To my horror, I'd spent more than four hours at the closet game.

"I'm home," Tony said. "I put in a full day without being paid a penny. I must be a saint."

"You are, Tony, you are. Did you get access to the cat area?"

"Briefly. Just had time to take a quick look around."

"Did you make contact?"

"Not really. But I'll do better tomorrow. There's an alcove on the second floor with a coffee machine. Everybody goes there. I'll hang around there."

"Good idea."

"The cat room is sort of off limits to most volunteers, looks like. They're paranoid in there."

"What do you mean?"

"They're scared of communicable diseases. There's been a lot of feline distemper around. Or so they tell me."

"Okay. That's understandable."

"But they like me there, Swede. They don't get too many real live male volunteers with hours and hours to kill." He laughed and added, "If only they knew."

"What time do you go in tomorrow?"

"Whenever I get up."

"Call me around lunchtime."

"Will do. But listen, Swede. Why don't we finish this off quick!"

"What?"

"What I mean is, why can't I just grab a few people and ask them about Jake?"

"No, no, you can't do that, Tony. Keep your mouth shut about Jake!" I was literally shouting into the phone.

"Who the hell do you think you're talking to like that?"

"I'm sorry, Tony."

"You can get some other idiot to play your games, lady."

"Please, Tony, I said I was sorry."

"Okay, okay. Let's both calm down, then."

"Yes, you're right."

Luckily, he was laughing again. "After all, we're lovers, aren't we?"

"Yes. And long-time companions," I added to the refrain.

"And theatrical comrades in arms."

"Exactly."

"That's our theme song now, so don't forget it."

He hung up. I stared at the shopping bags spilling over with clothing. Now they seemed irredeemably stupid. The conversation with Basillio had exhausted me. I was ashamed of my outburst. Imagine, shouting at poor Tony that way. Why on earth had I done that? Hadn't I read enough espionage novels to know that an undercover agent's "control" had to be a kindly, supportive, nonemotional individual?

Chapter 11

Day two in Tony Basillio's career as an undercover agent was uneventful. I guess the same could be said for my day. I was up for a voice-over job, but the audition was canceled.

Day three was almost as unremarkable for Tony, except that he expressed extreme displeasure with two of the dogs he had had to walk. One, he claimed, was a sexually aggressive boxer who kept trying to mount his leg.

Day four told the tale. Tony hit it big. I should have guessed it would be such, for the day broke cold, clear, crisp as rye toast, and the sun had that winter dazzle: it blinded and refreshed and strengthened you.

At eleven-thirty that morning, Tony called. He was, in spite of himself, excited.

"Know where I am?" he asked.

"No. Where?"

"A pay phone on First Avenue, right around the corner from Abide. Know where I was the last two hours?"

"No. Tell."

"In the cat room, helping out. They were passing out the pills."

"Good boy, Tony."

"I got what you want, Swede."

My fingers closed tightly around the receiver.

Tony was cackling now. "That's right. I got what you want."

"The witches of Endor, right?"

"Precisely. Like you said, there are three of them."

"Can you describe them?"

"Yeah. I even took notes."

I heard a rustling of paper. Then he gave me rather elaborate descriptions of the three women volunteers in the cat room. They sounded like the ladies Amanda and I had dealt with, but I couldn't be positive.

"Names, Tony, I need names."

"Sis Norlich."

"Right! Yes, I remember her."

"Ollie Hanner. That's the second one."

"Yes. Yes."

"And the third one . . . I couldn't get the full name. Jill something."

It was this third, partial name that really opened the

floodgates of memory. Jill was the one who had spoken those magic words—that Jake was "something of a problem."

It therefore had to be Jill who knew that Jake was Willie Sutton.

It therefore had to be Jill who murdered Amanda Avery, motive unknown.

Of course, everything was vague. Everything was connected by very tenuous strands.

One could say, So what if she said those words? So what if she knew Jake was Willie Sutton? How did that prove she kidnapped Jake and murdered Amanda after the ransom was paid? Was Jake really kidnapped? Or had he simply escaped and been collected?

I didn't care if it was all vague and tenuous. I *knew* it was Jill.

"Listen to me, Tony. What time does this Jill leave Abide?"

"I think all three leave sometime after four in the afternoon. The public isn't admitted after three-thirty."

"Okay. I want you to follow her."

"Which one, Jill?"

"Yes."

"Why her?"

"Because she's the one, Tony."

"The killer?"

"Yes."

"How do you know?"

"I know. Trust me."

"I'm running out of coins, Swede."

"Fine. Go now. Just follow her after she leaves work. Find out where she lives, what she does at night. Give me a flavor."

"Butter pecan."

I ignored the attempt at humor. "Follow her. Find out anything you can. If you think you can get even closer than that, ask her to have coffee with you."

"Are you kidding? I'm supposed to ask her out on a date? Is that what you're saying?"

The metal-tinged recorded voice interrupted us then, loudly demanding that Tony deposit more money. While he was explaining that he had no nickels in his pocket, we were disconnected.

Something of a problem. Something of a problem.

I kept repeating the words to myself after I got off the phone. Those words had been said to Amanda and said only by Jill. I was sure my memory was accurate in this matter. Those words differentiated her from the other volunteers. They marked her. They made her a legitimate suspect.

But what if all three of the volunteers had formed some kind of strange catnapping cabal?

Nothing was clear. But the simplest line of music is always the best. The killer came from Abide. Jill was the most likely suspect. Simple. Elegant. True.

As for motive: money? True, the usual kidnap/murder involved a great deal more money than was at stake in this case. Still, fifteen thousand dollars is not chicken feed.

As for the selection of the victim: Chance?

And the murder itself? Inexplicable.

I spent an agitated afternoon and early evening waiting for Tony. I didn't want to leave the apartment for a moment. I ate crackers and cheese and drank instant coffee. I read a few chapters of the only Virginia Woolf novel I could find on my bookshelf. Not *Mrs. Dalloway* . . . *To the Lighthouse*. That one I had never been able to finish—brilliant but exceedingly depressing.

This time I got through three chapters before putting it aside.

At one point, late in the afternoon, I must confess the pressure made me act a bit silly.

I started writing ditties based on the Frankie and Johnny legend. One of them went like this:

> *Jilly and Jake-O were sweethearts*
> *Lordy, how those two could love*
> *Then Jake took up with Amanda*
> *And Jill measured her for a shrove.*

I declaimed that one to Bushy, who listened noncommittally.

I was saved from further ditty nonsense by a call from

my friend Nora. Usually when she calls me in the afternoon she is a bit hysterical, having just finished the lunch shift at Pal Joey, and is getting ready for the evening crush.

This afternoon, however, my favorite restaurateur seemed low-keyed and even rather sad.

"Are you mad at me, Alice?"

"Of course not."

"Well, you haven't called or dropped by in quite a while."

"I've been really busy."

"How's Tony?"

"He's fine."

"Funny thing happened today, Alice. I learned something."

"Then it was a good day."

"I suppose you can say that. Actually, lunch was slow, so I spent a lot of time by the bar. Anyway, about one o'clock, two well-dressed gentlemen come in for drinks. They order a bottle of champagne at the bar. Not so common in my place, especially at lunchtime. And then guess what?"

"They start singing 'La Marseillaise'?"

"No. They begin talking about the theater."

"Well, Nora, your place *is* in the theater district."

There was a long silence. Then she began to speak in a tremulous, hurt-sounding voice. "I thought you were my friend, Alice. Why didn't you tell me?"

"Tell you what? Nora, what are you talking about?"

Nora burst into uproarious laughter then. "You didn't tell me that my friend Alice Nestleton . . . kind, good, elegant, slim, classical thespian that she is . . . engaged in lewd and lascivious displays for money on a public stage."

"I beg your pardon."

"Come on. Confess. Out with it. I have the goods."

"You've lost me, Nora."

"Oh, have I? Well, these two gentlemen, theater buffs obviously, were reminiscing about years past. One of them mentioned a sex play—oh yes, that's what he called it— that he saw some years ago off-off Broadway. It was called *The Divan* and it starred a toothsome blonde vamp named Eccleston."

I became a little lightheaded at the mention of that title. Yes, I remembered *The Divan*.

Nora gave one of her stage sighs. "I go on listening to Champagne Charlie," she said. "He begins to describe this actress Eccleston, and soon—oh, very soon, dearie—I realize he is talking about none other than one Alice Nestleton, a.k.a. the Swede, a.k.a. the Cat Woman."

Then she let out a fabulous whoop. "Alice, how dare you keep such a delicious tidbit from your old friend Nora."

"I hate to throw cold water on your salacious appetite, Nora. Yes, I was in that play. It ran for three weekends at a tiny theater on Barrow Street and then closed. But a sex play? Hardly. The subtitle of the thing was *The Secret Life of Madame Bovary*. It was a farce with a capital 'F.' Do you understand, Nora? A farce! Your gentleman quaffer has a fuzzy memory. Maybe he and his friend had champagne at five other bistros before they wandered into Pal Joey."

I didn't know if she was listening to a word I said. "I am crushed," she announced. "But I forgive you."

She hung up. And the clock started ticking. By the time the hour reached ten I had the feeling that Tony would not show; that some unexpected obstacle had risen out of the void and thwarted my chief undercover man.

I was wrong. The downstairs bell went off at twenty minutes to eleven. Tony fairly bounded up the stairs and into the loft.

He looked strange, wild. "Are you drunk, Basillio?"

He laughed. "Drunk? Yes. But not with alcohol, fair maiden. With you . . . on you." And then he grabbed me and waltzed me around the place. The dance ended quickly, since there was no music and I was a bit unwilling—and I did not have my dancing shoes on.

I sat down. He stood directly in front of me. His face was red from street wind and the dancing. He grinned.

"I'm waiting," I said.

He launched into a mock surveillance report: "Suspect left the building at 4:35 P.M. She walked north on First Avenue. At approximately 4:45 P.M. suspect entered the park just north of the United Nations. She proceeded past the 'St. George Slays the Missiles' statue, entered a path on the eastern edge of said park, and sat down on the third bench from the perimeter fence.

"Suspect then proceeded to remove a quasi-spherical object from her shoulder bag. I immediately identified it as an apple. She bit into object twelve times, removing flesh and masticating. Suspect then flung remains of object into wire trash basket and proceeded north again on First Avenue. Time was then approximately five-eighteen.

"Suspect then, obviously indifferent to her personal safety, walked over the Fifty-Ninth Street Bridge. Fully cognizant of my duties, and in spite of the dangers, I maintained surveillance.

"Once off the bridge, suspect walked toward Queens Boulevard and entered the main building of La Guardia Community College. At this point, contact was broken off."

He bowed. Granted, it was an amazing performance, and at first I really didn't know what to say. So I opted for compassion: "Are you tired, Basillio? Do you want some tea? Coffee? Something to eat?"

"No, thank you."

"Well, you did a remarkable job of surveillance. I'm sorry she led you over the bridge. I know you don't like heights. And if I recall, that bridge's walking path has, at least for part of it, a steel web floor. You can look through it down to the water below."

"My heart is pure, Swede. I have the strength of ten."

"But the problem is—and I'm sure you'll agree—you found out nothing related to the case."

He waved his hands furiously, as if swatting flies.

"What I found, Alice, is so startling, so beautiful, that our world can be transformed."

"You're confusing me, Tony."

He knelt down beside me and lay his head on my knee for a moment.

"Are you ill, Tony?"

He threw back his head with a furious laugh. "Yes, I'm ill with beauty and love. Let me tell you what I really saw."

"Please do."

"I took a bus back across the bridge, figuring I would then take the Second Avenue bus home. But I could see there was bad traffic on the avenue because of some Con Edison repairs, so I decided to walk back downtown on First and then cut back to Second at around Forty-Second Street.

"Of course, I end up passing that U.N. park again. At that hour it was closed, so I passed it on the street. Suddenly my eye caught on an astonishingly beautiful flower. Am I going mad? I thought. The flower was delicate, rich, yellow, perfectly formed. I moved closer. I pressed my face against the fence.

"Just inside was a small puddle of muck and mud. Floating in the mess were some green stems, and on those stems were *five* dazzling yellow water lilies.

"They were so strange and so magnificent that I lurched backwards as if I had been struck. Then I moved close again and I realized they were simply unlike any other flowers I had ever seen in my life. They were perfectly formed. The color was like the sun. They . . ."

He stopped talking suddenly, as if he could not properly articulate his emotions.

"You sound like you've had a vision, a religious conversion," I noted dryly, thinking about Harry Bondo and his ducks and hoping that this conversion would not turn Tony into a vegetarian. "But Tony," I added gently, "I sincerely don't think they were water lilies."

"Why not? Because this is Manhattan? Because it's late fall? But that's the wonder of it, Swede. Don't you see? The sheer, sudden, sublime, spectacular mystery of it. A stage design created by a phantom, signifying everything."

My! He certainly was waxing poetic. For a minute there, I thought perhaps his two love-giving cats, Tiny and Tim, had been working on him again. Once before, their magic had made a rose-sniffing, poem-spouting fool of him.

"Let us reason together," I said, using an old phrase of my grandmother's that she used when I did something wrong and she was trying very hard to find the patience not to paddle me.

"Reason is the last refuge of a turkey vulture," he replied.

I ignored his cryptic aphorism.

Lydia Adamson

"First of all, Tony, it is too late in the year for water lilies in the Northeast. Secondly, it is simply too cold. Third, and most important, the flowers of yellow water lilies, if I recall, bloom only in the daytime. They recede at night."

"I am impressed by your botanical knowledge, but I saw what I saw."

Then he grasped my hand hard. "Let me show them to you!"

"I'll walk by when I get a chance."

"No, now! Right now!"

"Please, Tony. It's late. We're both tired."

He bolted away from me, throwing his hands up in disgust.

"Listen! I volunteered for you. I walked those hounds for you. I followed that Jill for you. I walked across that damn bridge for you . . . high up . . . over dark, dangerous waters. And what do I get? Nothing. I ask you for one lousy favor. To accompany me to see something beautiful. What kind of relationship is this? Am I your damn slave? When do you do one single thing for me that even begins to reciprocate what I do for you?"

I had never seen him quite like that before. I felt absolutely miserable. He was right. Reciprocity was not our strong point. He extended himself for me so much more, and so much more often, than I did for him.

"Very well, Tony," I responded softly, "show me the yellow water lilies."

I threw on a coat and followed him down the stairs and onto the street. He grasped my hand as we hailed a cab, saying, "You won't be sorry." He didn't release my hand until the cab dropped us on First Avenue and Forty-sixth Street.

Then he took my arm and escorted me to the fence from which one could peer through and down into his enchanted puddle.

"There!" he announced triumphantly. At last he dropped my arm.

I stared at the brackish little puddle. There wasn't a single lily floating on it . . . not a single flower of any kind . . . not a speck of yellow or any other brightness. Just dull gray and brown.

I turned to him. "There's nothing, Tony. Are you sure this is the right puddle?"

He was smiling.

"What's so bloody funny?"

"How did I do, Swede?" he asked airily. "A good acting job?"

I exploded. "You mean all this was a fake? A practical joke?"

He started to walk away. I followed him, shouting, accusing, growing more and more furious at his idiocy.

He walked faster, following the park fence, rounding the corner, heading toward the river. I kept after him. I kept shouting.

Suddenly he stopped on a dime and faced me. "You've lost your sense of humor, Swede."

"Do you really consider this funny?"

"But there were extenuating circumstances."

"Like what?"

"Let me show you."

"More invisible water lilies?"

"Not exactly."

Gently, he pulled me close to the fence again.

"Take a look," he said. He was pointing to a long rectangular patch of ivy between the fence and an interior path.

"What?"

"Keep looking."

I stared into the dark tangle of ivy. I saw nothing. "Take me home, Tony. I'm not mad anymore, just weary."

"Keep looking, little girl," he said, his voice high and squeaky, sounding like the good witch from *The Wizard of Oz*.

Then I saw a ripple: the wind whipping the ivy, I supposed.

Then I saw a shadow.

Finally I saw the living shape of a cat.

"Oh my God, Tony. It's Jake!"

The harlequin cat sat straight up in the ivy bed, resplendent in his brown and black bifurcation. He stared at us through the rungs of the fence.

"So," Tony said coolly, "do we figure out a way to grab him?"

"No," I cautioned.

"What then?"

"Wait."

I pressed my face against the fence. "Are you well, Jake?" I called.

He yawned in answer.

"We'll leave him for now, Tony," I said. "Let's go to Amanda's place. It's only a few blocks away."

The walk took place in silence. Once we were inside, I flicked on the light and immediately sat down. The place seemed so empty and strange without Good Girl.

"You look pale, Swede."

"I imagine I do."

"Hey, I'm sorry I pulled that stuff," Tony said earnestly. "I don't know what got into me. I should have just told you straight out that I found the cat. I think I was mad at you for having to walk over that bridge. The yellow water lilies were a stupid kind of payback. I'm sorry."

I closed my eyes. Jake was alive and well. That was what really counted. But just seeing him had really drained me, particularly after my emotional outburst against Tony for the water lily debacle.

"Guess you're tired, huh? We could sleep here," Tony said happily. "I think it could be fun."

"You'll be having fun alone," I replied, opening my eyes.

"Is there a refrigerator here?"

I pointed in the direction of the kitchen. He walked in there, opened the fridge, then slammed it shut again. "Empty."

"Sit down a minute, Tony."

"But I'm hungry."

"Just for a minute, Tony!"

"Okay. Why not?"

"Do you realize what has happened?"

"No. Enlighten me."

"Jake was never kidnapped. He got out of here—somehow—when Amanda was taking care of him, just as he got out while I was taking care of him."

"Um."

"He went to that U.N. park after he got loose. Maybe it's one of the places he always went after he pulled an escape. Like Willie Sutton, he has safe houses all over the city. Jake's a slick one. And this Jill knows his pattern. She just kept a watch because she knew he'd get out of here. She found him but she didn't return him even though she knew full well where he belonged. Nor did she return him to Abide. Why should she?

"Here was a way to extort fifteen thousand dollars. Amanda thought the cat had been kidnapped. Amanda thought he was in danger. Do you understand, Tony?"

"Jill is pretty slick herself," he said. "She must have planned it carefully."

"Not *too* carefully. It could only work when and if Jake escaped."

"But he always did."

"Yes."

"Let's face it. The woman is home free, Swede. You can't get her for catnapping, because there was no catnapping. You can't get her for murder; the cops have no prints and no real witnesses."

"You're right. But maybe she'll strike again."

"Why would she do that?"

"Because she's greedy, that's why. And because Jake is available again."

"I'm not following."

"What if Jake was adopted by another rich man's widow?"

"But . . . but how? How can he be adopted by anybody? He's loose now."

"What if this mythical rich widow walks into Abide and asks for Jake, or a cat just like him?"

"You mean, Jill Baby goes to the park, collects her sidekick Jake, and starts the whole cycle again."

"That's what I mean."

"That's brilliant, Swede. And this time we know what's going to happen. We stop it. And we get Jill with the goods, so to speak."

"Exactly."

He raised a cautionary hand. "But the only rich guy's widow you knew is dead."

"True. But what about a rich woman's husband—a widower."

"You know one?"

"No. But we can create one, can't we?"

He looked puzzled, and I let him remain that way for the present. All would be clear by noon the following day, when Tony and I would be paying a visit to Sam Tully.

Before we left Amanda's apartment, Tony said, "I hate to bring this up, Madam Nestleton, but did it ever occur to you that Jake is an accessory to murder?"

Chapter 12

Is this a social call?" Sam asked. "I'm out of tea and crumpets." He was at his typewriter.

His animosity toward Tony, which was entirely mutual, seemed to overwhelm him for a moment. But then he graciously choked it back.

Of course, I had carefully prepped Tony as to how to act . . . in other words, "No sneering, and keep your mouth shut unless you need to go to the bathroom."

I smiled. Pickles was not on the roof today, even though the windows onto the fire escape were wide open; he was sprawled on the table next to the typewriter.

Good Girl was snoozing in a chair, twitching and dreaming, her long ears like rag-mop black and tan pendulums.

Pages were scattered on the floor around the typewriter.

165

Harry Bondo must have been in the middle of some psychosexual cataclysm.

"It is definitely not a social call," I said. "I need your help again, Sam."

"That's my middle name, honey," he said. Then he scooped up the papers from the floor, shuffled them together, and slid them under the typewriter carriage. He lit a cigarette and blew smoke toward the ceiling.

"We found Jake, Sam. He's living quite happily on his own, in a park near the U.N. And we found Amanda's murderer. She's one of the volunteers at Abide. And we know how she operates."

"You've been a busy gal," Sam noted.

"Now we want to flush her out. To put her into motion again."

"You mean you wanna sucker her, right? Like a sting."

"Yes, that's it. We must present her with something so appetizing that she'll have to act. And where you come in is—well, we want you to adopt Jake, in a way."

"Whoa!" he exploded. "No good, doll. I got Pickles and Good Girl. I can't handle no more. Besides, you just said Jake is living the life of Riley in the park."

"Correct. And when the killer finds out you want Jake, she'll go to that park, collect him, give him to you under the auspices of Abide, wait until he escapes, claim it's a kidnapping, and demand a ransom for his return."

Tony spoke for the first time. "You don't ask for Jake by

name, of course. That would blow the whole thing. You just don't want any of their current crop. You tell them you want something different . . . wild cat . . . crazy cat . . . bizarre feline of some sort . . . one with a dazzling coat of colors. Get it?"

"And," I added, "you don't walk into Abide as Sam Tully."

"Definitely not," echoed Tony. Sam gave him a quick dirty look.

"If you agree to do this, Tully—and I hope very much you will—you'll go in as a wealthy eccentric, the widower of a woman who had a fortune. You know—throw hundred-dollar bills around; donate to this, donate to that; tip everybody you see. Okay?"

"Sure."

"So you understand what's happening?"

"Not really. To be honest, honey, I can't figure out what the hell you're talking about."

"Listen. We're trying to recreate the Ivan Tasso/Amanda Avery complex. Tasso left Amanda oodles of money. She didn't have to get her cat at a free adoption center. It was just in character for her to do so, since Ivan gave a lot of money to hospitals and clinics. I saw the canceled checks myself. You see, we're recreating the scenario, with a few alterations. This time it's the wife who has died, and the husband who is going to take in a cat because his wife always loved cats dearly, but the couple traveled too much to have one."

Sam's eyes lit up. "This is one wild scheme, doll. I gotta hand it to you."

"I had a feeling you would appreciate it."

"What's my name?"

"How about Brian Paup?"

"I don't like it at all," Tony chimed in.

"I love it," said Sam. "It's me."

"Good," I said.

"Clothes, doll. I need clothes. And a hairstylist!"

Sam was really getting into it. I had to squelch him quickly.

"No time for that, Sam. We're moving on this immediately. Now."

"Now? You mean today?"

"Yes. Abide closes at four. The volunteers leave. You have to be there by three o'clock. Go just as you are. You're supposed to be eccentric, remember. You look fine."

I motioned to Tony, using a prearranged signal. He handed an envelope to Sam.

"There are hundreds and fifties in here," I explained, "and a few twenties. I borrowed the cash from Nora and I'll pay back every cent. But you, Sam, you've got to just throw it around like scrap paper."

"That's fine with me," he said.

"So you'll do it?"

He ground out the cigarette. "Body and soul, honey. Body and soul."

"Sit down, Sam. This is probably your biggest role to date. I think I should help you a bit with the preparation."

"You mean like an acting lesson?"

"Sort of. But more a walk-through. Brian Paup enters Abide around three. A lot of bluster in his manner. But he's basically kindly. He goes to the receptionist's counter. Tells them he wants to adopt a cat. They'll send him—you—to an interviewer. Everyone who wants to adopt gets a short interview to ascertain if they're an ax murderer or something. You pass the test. Fine. But before you get interviewed, before you leave the receptionist's desk, you buy a lot of the Abide T-shirts and sweatshirts that are displayed on the counter. Start throwing money around right away. Establish your credentials. Understood?"

"Got it."

"Then they'll send you into the area where they keep the cats. Three volunteers will be on duty there. Jill is the one you want to connect with. Understood?"

"Got it. So far, it's a piece of cake."

"Now comes the subtle part. You look at all the available kitties. You start to get anxious. Oh, you say, they're all lovely, but I want something *really special*. A cat that will do justice to my dead wife.

"Then you confide in the cat handlers—tell them how much you loved her and how she was a very beautiful but strange lady with perhaps a warped personality. You might even break down in the telling. Think you can do that, Sam?"

"You mean tears and all?"

"Yes."

"I'll give it a shot."

For a moment I thought of the possibility of giving him one of those old-fashioned "Method" exercises where the acting students are jolted into weeping real tears, authentic tears. But I decided against it.

"Do I swagger in or saunter in?" Tully asked.

"Sauntering is better, I would think," I replied. "In other words, Sam, this Brian Paup is eccentric but not excessive—except when it comes to a cat."

"I think I see what the role's all about."

"Good, Sam."

"But listen, doll, I think I need something else."

"What do you mean? You want to construct a background for Paup? For instance, who was he before he met this wealthy late wife and where did all her dough come from?" I was impressed with the way Sam was approaching his role. I myself would have required that kind of information, at the very least, if there was time.

"No, I don't mean that," he said. "I mean, I need a hat."

"Hat?"

"Yeah. I think this guy should wear some kind of a wild hat. From my experience, rich jerks always wear a hat."

"He is *not* a jerk," Tony interjected angrily. "It's a profound misunderstanding of who this guy is to call him a jerk."

It was the wrong comment made at the wrong time. Sam and Tony began shouting at each other. The situation escalated from there. Finally, Sam threatened to throw Tony out of the apartment.

I interceded, calmed things down. I spoke gently to Sam and Tony, and even to Pickles and Good Girl, both of whom had been riveted to the heated argument. I told all parties how bright and wonderful they were. The roiled waters began to recede.

"Sam, I've been thinking," I said. "Upon reflection, I do believe a hat would be a good thing. See, I think Tony just doesn't quite understand that you come out of the Old Vic tradition. You know, the Stratford and London school, where the single most important element of stagecraft is a distinctive prop—an umbrella, a scarf, a cane, what have you. Am I right, Sam?"

"Right as rain, doll."

"What are our hat options?"

"Not much on hand," he admitted. He went to the nearest closet and retrieved a bedraggled collection: fishing hat, beret, baseball cap, derby, porkpie.

We studied them carefully from the perspective of the Brian Paup scenario. All animosities seemed to dissolve wondrously in the common enquiry. Finally it was decided that Tully a.k.a. Paup should saunter into Abide wearing a beret. He modeled it for us. Excellent! We were set—almost. It was one o'clock. I proceeded with final instructions.

"Tony will leave here shortly and go straight to Abide. He's undercover now, as an animal-loving volunteer. He walks dogs, primarily.

"You and I will leave here around two, Sam. You enter Abide at three. Naturally, you and Tony do not know each other. Naturally, neither of you should follow or make any kind of contact with Jill after she leaves the building.

"Both of you are to go to Amanda's apartment after you leave Abide. Tony has the key. Wait there for me. I'll find a little nook somewhere and stake out the park alone—oh, that reminds me, I need to borrow your Polaroid, Sam."

"You're going to have either a very short wait or a very long one," Tony noted. "Jill leaves at four-thirty, but it doesn't get dark until about five-thirty. If she sits in the park for a while eating an apple or whatever, like she did before, there'll still be some daylight left. Would she collect the cat while it was still light?"

"Why not?" I said. "It's just a stray. Who's going to care? Besides, if she doesn't get Jake then . . . then when? That park gets shut down at night. Maybe Jake can slip in and out, but not Jill."

"How late will you stay there?"

"If it doesn't happen right away, I'll keep skulking around the area until about nine. Then I'll call you at Amanda's and maybe one of you can spell me. But I'm afraid if nothing's happened by nine o'clock, it won't happen at all. We may have to forget the whole thing."

Tony left soon afterward to report for work. Sam ordered in a thin-crust pizza, which he paid for with a twenty-dollar bill from the envelope containing Brian Paup's wad. Then he made me coffee.

"You suppose this is how Finney 'prepares' for a part?" he asked. "Pizza and all?"

For a moment I hadn't the slightest idea who he meant. Then I realized he was talking about Albert Finney. "Somehow, I don't think so, Sam. But anything's possible."

I made a little adjustment of his beret on his old gray head. "Are you ready to go on, Sam?"

We were standing at the corner of Thirty-seventh Street and First Avenue. The wind was high and the traffic was light.

"Honest answer. I'm a little nervous. But yeah, I'm ready," Sam said.

"It's normal to be nervous, Sam. That's a good thing. As long as your neck isn't tight."

"No. My neck's good."

"Loose?"

"Yeah."

"Let's see."

He rotated his head easily, full circle.

"Okay. You're looking good, Sam. You know exactly who you are, right?"

"Sure. A crazy rich jerk named Brian Paup. I throw the bucks around like Raisinettes."

"Okay, Tully. Knock 'em dead."

He sauntered off, beret tilted at just the right insouciant angle.

I walked slowly to the park. A light drizzle had begun to fall. Once inside the main park gates, I was astonished to find that it was patrolled by uniformed men and women with guns. It had not occurred to me until then that this was not an ordinary New York City park, and the patrollers were not ordinary Parks Department personnel. No, they were United Nations police.

I followed the same route Jill had taken the evening Basillio tailed her: past Saint George and the Missiles, onto the path and then to the bench where she had sat enjoying an apple.

I sat down on the same bench, only I had no apple. Since I was still a bit hungry, it might not have been a bad idea to pick one up, I thought futilely. I saw the ivy patch, only a few yards away, where Tony and I had last sighted Jake. There were many other such patches. In fact, ivy seemed to be the horticultural motif of the area.

The rain was coming down with a bit more force now. I wrapped my shawl around my head then (too bad I hadn't borrowed one of Tully's hats) and walked out of the park by the side gate, heading up First Avenue. I found a coffee shop and ordered a hot chocolate. The brew itself was pretty tasty, but I took my spoon and shaved off the fake whipped cream floating on the top.

At four o'clock I went back to the park and stationed myself across the street from the fence and Jake's ivy patch. I kept my eyes peeled for him, but he did not show. Well, that wasn't so peculiar—feral cats prefer nocturnal settings.

The street on which I was waiting was a dead end running smack up against an abandoned and closed-off exit ramp from the East River Drive. Behind me was the trash collection plaza of an elegant old building—just a concrete lot from building line to street.

If Lady Jill was going to eat her apple on that bench and then collect Jake with an eye to more perfidy, it would have to be soon. Daylight was beginning to fade.

She did not show before evening fell. At five-thirty I watched the U.N. cops lock all the gates to the park and bid one another good night.

I settled down for the long haul, shivering even though I was in my good wool coat. My eyes were fixed on First Avenue. Jill would have to come from that direction now that the park was locked up. I was reaching that bad moment that inevitably came when a stakeout was taking longer than it should—when an investigation was generally going sour. It was the moment when my self-confidence began to desert me and I began to feel like a bit of a fool.

I was now walking back and forth, tracing the four corners of a small rectangle. At six-thirty I started humming snatches of dance tunes—inane 1970s disco songs that I could only dimly recall, since I had been at so few discos in my life. I remembered the pounding, monotonous beat, but rarely the words.

A few passersby, mostly folks out strolling with their dogs, glanced at me with suspicion. I can't say I blame them; I *was* loitering, and I *was* singing "Do the Hustle." But no one said anything and no cops appeared to order me to move along.

I wondered if Tony and Sam were both back at Amanda's by now. If so, I hoped they were getting along, tolerating each other, at the very least. It would be terrible—shameful—if they came to blows and wrecked what was left of Amanda's home. That would be like speaking ill of the dead.

Had Sam been able to pull off the wealthy eccentric act, or had he lost control and reverted to a Harry Bondo mode?

I began to worry about Bushy and Poncho—whether they had enough to eat, whether there was enough heat in the loft, and so on. Worrying about stuff like that, I knew, meant I was truly losing heart and losing focus. I silently cursed my weakness and began to go over the puzzle again.

Yes, damn it. I *was* in the right place. Yes, it was the right time. Yes, I was waiting for the right murderess. Yes, the trap had been set well. Yes, yes, it was going to clang shut on the killer.

The rain was lighter now, but the wind off the river had picked up. I was standing in almost total darkness. The merest shard of street light meandered from a point behind me, over the ground, and licked at the park fence.

The world was genuinely black and white now. I suddenly had the feeling that I was in an old movie about New York gangsters. I was Lilli Palmer (maybe you prefer Jean Peters? Valentina Cortese?). I was waiting for Richard Conte (Widmark? Victor Mature?). I grinned, almost obscenely.

And then, right then, with the grin still on my face, I saw a figure turn off the avenue and walk slowly east quite close to the fence. I was reminded of the way a child rakes a stick along a picket fence as she passes by it.

This wasn't just any figure, either. It was a female form. And she was wearing a dark cloak with the hood up!

I stood absolutely still. I could hear my heartbeat. I could for some reason taste salt on my tongue. The fingers of my right hand involuntarily grasped the Polaroid.

She stopped just in front of the ivy patch. From beneath the cloak she took out a sheet of paper and began to crinkle it loudly. A trick, I realized, to get Jake's attention. Many cats respond to a sound like that. She waited. So did I.

I caught some movement in the ivy. Was it Jake?

She removed another object from her pocket. It was a tube of some kind. She unscrewed the top of it and then bent down.

There he was! I could see Jake clearly. He was approaching her through the ivy like a carriage horse trotting through brambles.

Now! I thought. It has to be now. I took a deep breath and swiftly crossed the street.

Stopping just three feet behind her, I called out: "Amanda Avery sends her regrets." I had not planned to say such a harsh and bitter thing, and I don't know why those particular words came to me. They just did.

She whirled, turning her delicate, pale face to me. My words seemed to have paralyzed her. I pointed the camera dead in her face and snapped the shutter.

Nothing!

I jammed my finger down furiously on the button again. Nothing! No response at all. The bloody thing would not work. It was broken. I flung it to the ground in disgust.

Then and only then did I realize that the woman crouched at the fence was not the volunteer whose name was Jill. Nor was she any of the other workers from the Abide cat room.

But I did know the woman. From somewhere. I knew who this slim, dark woman was . . . but I could not remember. Her identity, her name, was floating somewhere at the outer reaches of my memory.

She bolted like a frightened wild animal then, streaking past me. But she was running the wrong way. She was heading toward the river and soon found herself facing a concrete abutment.

I picked up the tube I had seen her uncap. It was Petro-malt. The medicinal paste recommended for cat hairballs. If your cat doesn't like it, it can be a pain in the neck to get it down his gullet. But many cats love the taste of it madly—more than grisly sardines—more than catnip.

Jake was in his ivy patch, a mere foot away from the fence. His strange bifurcated coat made him look like two distinct creatures. His eyes were riveted on the Petromalt.

I turned and stared at the frightened woman. I was suddenly suffused with a strange glow. I knew who she was now.

This was the volunteer who had interviewed Amanda Avery. She was Abide's Intake Interviewer.

And then the glow turned to self-loathing. Of course. How stupid I had been! It was the interviewer alone who knew that Amanda had money . . . that she was a wealthy widow.

"It's too late now," I said. "It's all over."

She did not speak. She was trembling.

I didn't recall the young woman's name, but I now knew who she was and I certainly knew what she had done. So I lied boldly and without qualms. I lied, as the saying goes, like a thief.

"Believe me," I told her, taking another step closer, "it's useless to try to get away. We know everything. You've been followed since the night of the murder. The police have found an eyewitness. The moment you turned the corner I called the homicide detectives. As we stand here, they are heading toward your apartment with a search warrant. They will get in by any means necessary. And they will find the money—whatever there is left of it. Do you think Amanda was a fool? Don't you know that she marked the bills? It's all over!"

She watched my lips move. The tears were rolling down her face. But I never let up.

"You were going to trap Brian Paup the way you trapped Amanda Avery. Weren't you? You were going to wait till Willie Sutton got out and then extort money for his safe return. We know everything, like I said. We know how you work."

"No! No!" It was a plaintive cry.

"Were you going to slaughter that old man as well? Like you killed Amanda Avery?"

"No! Believe me. It was a mistake. It wasn't supposed to happen like that."

"Why did you kill her?"

Her words came out in a pathetic torrent. "I didn't mean to. I didn't want to hurt her at all. I knew immediately who her husband was. People thought he had been a philanthropist. I knew different. I knew him as a butcher. I knew he gave money to research centers that tortured cats on the grounds that they were enhancing human health.

"But I didn't plan anything. I was just walking past the park and saw the cat. And I realized he had escaped from Amanda Avery's. I thought how wonderful and just it would be if I could get some of Ivan Tasso's money and use it *for* cats instead of against them. I was going to give all the money away. Don't you understand?"

She reached into her pocket then. I stepped back, suddenly afraid. Did she have the same kind of screwdriver she'd used on Amanda? Or was it a gun this time?

But no. She threw two cans of cat food onto the ground between us.

"I heard Jake was back in his old haunts, so I came here tonight to feed him. And to apologize for what happened."

"You're apologizing to a cat?"

"For the horror that he had to witness. Avery brought the money. She gave it to me. I turned Jake over to her. But I couldn't keep silent. I had to tell her why I was doing what I was doing. I had to tell her what her husband's money bought—the misery it caused. She defended him. She began to curse me, called me an idiot. I carried the screwdriver because it was a bad neighborhood and I wanted to be able to defend myself. I had no idea of hurting her. But then she called me all those things and was walking away from me. I could see Jake's face over her shoulder. And I thought of all those cats—violated, tortured, imprisoned. And for what? To test cosmetics? To try out blood thinners that might someday be useful to phlebitis sufferers? I just went crazy, I guess. I don't know why or how. I took the thing in both my hands and I . . ."

Breaking into sobs, she could not finish. It didn't matter, though.

Her name, it turned out, was Cora Iturbi. And the odd denouement was that I had to help her walk to Amanda Avery's apartment, where, an hour later, she was cuffed and read her rights by Detectives Webster and Luboff, then bundled into a police vehicle and taken away.

Tony, Sam, and I remained in the apartment. I was exhausted. Tony went out and brought back coffee and toasted muffins.

"If you believe her, Swede, and she was just going to the park to feed Jake because she found out he was there again, then the whole elaborate trap was worthless. Do you know what I'm saying? She was there because she was there. It had nothing to do with Mr. Brian Paup's visit to Abide."

"You're talking through your hat, buster," said Sam.

"Tony," Basillio corrected him icily. "The name is Tony."

"Yeah, yeah. There's an old saying: When two water buffalo collide, a mosquito dies."

"What does that have to do with anything we're talking about here?" Tony demanded.

Tully smirked. "It's too deep for you, kid."

"Tony. I told you, my name is Tony."

"Gentlemen," I said, interceding, "would it be possible to finish the evening on a note of peace and calm? It doesn't really matter what cause triggered what effect. We found who we were looking for. We found Amanda's killer."

"Looking back," Tony said, "it had to be the interviewer, didn't it?"

"What are you going to do with the cat?" asked Sam.

"Leave him," I stated.

"What?"

"You heard me," I reiterated. "I am going to leave Jake exactly where he is."

"But winter's coming."

"And after winter, the spring. Let's face it, Jake wants to be outside—free, prowling. I don't have a romantic view of alley cats. But in this case I think Jake has earned his freedom, as he comprehends it."

"Someone will pick him up again," Sam said. "Specially if his coat is as wild as you say."

And, I thought, if he's addicted to Petromalt. "You're probably right, Sam. By the way, how did it go at Abide?"

"How did it go? I dazzled 'em. They bought it hook, line, and sinker. I mean, when I was in that cat area giving them the spiel about my dead wife being so kookily beautiful that I had to find a feline to match her, their eyes filled up with tears. That's right—I had 'em crying. And take a look at this!"

He reached down and pulled an assortment of Abide logo T-shirts from a huge tote bag also bearing the logo.

"Yeah, I went through that cash you gave me like a hot knife through butter. The way you said I should do it. Got rid of it all."

He then began pulling out cat food and brushes and toys, and even, finally, several tubes of Petromalt.

I watched calmly. I was not at all surprised. I fell fast asleep with a muffin in my hand.

"Actually, I should have realized it wasn't one of the three volunteers in the cat room," I said to Detective Yvonne Webster, who was seated across from me at the coffee shop on Hudson Street, just a few blocks from my loft. Luboff was outside in the double-parked vehicle.

It was a beautiful morning and I was being quite open with Detective Webster because she had asked me to have some breakfast with her in order to thank me. I hadn't expected such a chivalrous offer.

"You mean," she said, "because it is the interviewer who gets financial data on the adopters."

"Not that alone. I mean, it's probably quite common for the interviewer to relay choice bits of information to the rest of the staff. I'm talking about the gloves."

"What about them?"

"Anyone who knew Jake intimately knew that handling gloves were never required with him. He wouldn't scratch anyone."

"Do you believe what Iturbi said about apologizing to this Jake character? Do you believe she showed up just to feed the cat and apologize to it?"

"Hard to say."

"How do you apologize to a cat, anyway?"

"There are many ways. Particularly if one becomes obsessed with the issue of animals in medical research."

"But you went there because you thought she was going to work the same scam with that old guy you sent into Abide."

"Exactly."

She laughed for a long time.

"What's so funny?" I asked, feeling tense for the first time that morning.

"I've been a cop for sixteen years and a detective for seven of them. And I never saw a piece of police work that started out so crazy and ended up so well."

"Are you complimenting me or insulting me?"

"Drink your coffee, Alice. You don't mind if I call you Alice? What I'm saying is that I now know those people downtown knew what the hell they were talking about. You really are the Cat Woman."

She slid out of the booth and stood up. The butt of her weapon was visible on her belt. Then she waggled a finger at me, Dutch uncle style.

"What?" I said.

"One day you're going to get involved with some characters who will hurt you."

"I guess so."

"And then the fun and games will be all over."

I laughed.

"You find that amusing, Alice?"

"No. It's just that I think the fun and games ended for me when I left Minnesota to become an actress. And that was a long time ago."

"That really where you're from?"

"Right. A little old dairy farm owned and run by a little old lady—my grandmother."

"So you know your way around a cow?"

"You bet I do."

"You folks make any cheese there?"

"Once in a while."

Yvonne Webster gave a gentle sigh. "You may not believe this, but I always wanted to milk a real live cow. Just walk into a big old barn and sit down on one of those wooden stools, pull up a pail with a wire handle, and milk a real cow."

What could I say to that! We shook hands, firmly, and she left.

I dallied over my coffee. And I thought of Jake.

Jake the cat. Jake the hostage. Jake the escape artist. Jake the resident alien of the U.N. park. Jake the harlequin. Jake the accessory to murder.

And then I had a wild fantasy—of the district attorney calling on Jake to testify against Cora Iturbi. And his refusing to answer questions on the grounds that the answers might incriminate him.

I just sat there and purred. Like Clarissa Dalloway.